Phoebe

thought she'd had her fill of dealing with demon romance when she fell for Cole Turner. Now she's a pawn in a supernatural love connection.

Paige

is feeling the badness-busting burnout. But an attempt to get in touch with her inner party girl could be the undoing of the Power of Three.

Piper

wants the Charmed Ones to learn more about Wiccan tradition. Unfortunately, a mysterious power outage forces her to redirect her attention—and rethink the consequences of her future with Leo.

The Charmed Ones have a story for every season!

D1331631

Seasons of
the Witch, Vol.1

More titles in the

Pocket Books series

THE POWER OF THREE
KISS OF DARKNESS
THE CRIMSON SPELL
WHISPERS FROM THE PAST
VOODOO MOON
HAUNTED BY DESIRE
THE GYPSY ENCHANTMENT
THE LEGACY OF MERLIN
SOUL OF THE BRIDE
BEWARE WHAT YOU WISH
CHARMED AGAIN
SPIRIT OF THE WOLF
DATE WITH DEATH
GARDEN OF EVIL
DARK VENGEANCE
SHADOW OF THE SPHINX
SOMETHING WICCAN THIS WAY COMES
MIST AND STONE
MIRROR IMAGE
BETWEEN WORLDS
TRUTH AND CONSEQUENCES
LUCK BE A LADY
INHERIT THE WITCH

All Pocket Books are available by post from:
Simon & Schuster Cash Sales. PO Box 29
Douglas, Isle of Man IM99 1BQ
Credit cards accepted.
Please telephone 01624 836000
fax 01624 670923
Internet http://www.bookpost.co.uk
or email: bookshop@enterprise.net for details

Seasons of
the Witch, Vol. 1

Based on the hit TV series created by

Constance M. Burge

Simon & Schuster, London

First published in Great Britain in 2004 by Simon & Schuster UK Ltd.
Africa House, 64–78 Kingsway, London WC2B 6AH
A Viacom Company.

Originally published in 2003 by Simon Pulse,
an imprint of Simon & Schuster Children's Division, New York

™ & © 2003 by Spelling Television Inc. All Rights Reserved.

A CIP catalogue record for this book is available from the British Library
upon request.

ISBN 0 6898 7271 2

3 5 7 9 10 8 6 4 2

Printed in Great Britain by
Cox & Wyman Ltd, Reading, Berkshire

Samhain

by Laura J. Burns

"Trick or treat!"

Phoebe Halliwell smiled down at the pack of little goblins on the doorstep of the manor house she shared with her sisters. "Yeow! You guys are scary!" she told them, filling their pumpkin head baskets with candy.

"Thank you!" they chorused, trooping back down the stairs.

Phoebe took a deep breath of late-afternoon autumn air and turned back inside. She loved Halloween. It had been her favorite holiday ever since she was a little girl playing dress up. And now that she was a full-grown witch, she loved it even more.

Phoebe made her way into the big kitchen, where her older sister, Piper, was making soup in a giant pot.

"Practicing your chef skills?" Phoebe asked.

"Leo's been working long hours lately," Piper replied. "I thought I'd make him a nice home-cooked meal to cheer him up."

"His charges are always in trouble around this time of year, huh?" Phoebe said.

"You know it," Piper replied.

"Am I missing something?" asked Paige, their younger half sister, as she wandered into the kitchen. "Why would Leo's charges be in trouble? Is there some big monster thingie I should know about?"

Phoebe grinned. Paige was still new at being a Charmed One. Phoebe and Piper had known for years now about their Wiccan heritage, but Paige had discovered it only recently. "No monster," Phoebe told Paige. "Just Samhain."

"What did you just say?" Paige asked. "Sow'n?"

"Today is Samhain," Phoebe said. "It's a sort of New Year's celebration for witches."

"And for all sorts of demons, warlocks, and mischievous spirits," Piper added dryly. "Demons love a good party."

"So you mean all those ghosts and ghouls out there trick-or-treating might actually *be* ghosts and ghouls?" Paige asked.

Phoebe nodded. "The days leading up to Halloween, or Samhain, are always filled with extra-magical happenings. That's because Samhain is the day on which the veil between our world and the world of the dead is thinnest. So evil spirits can slip through." She hesitated. "Or good spirits."

Piper narrowed her eyes. "What are you up to?" she asked.

"Nothing," Phoebe answered, trying to sound as innocent as possible. But it was useless. She could never lie to Piper. The doorbell rang. "More little monsters! I'll get it!" Phoebe grabbed the bowl of Halloween candy and spun toward the front door.

"Stop!" Piper called.

Phoebe stopped. *Busted.*

Piper came over and took the bowl out of Phoebe's arms. "Paige, would you get the door?" she asked. Paige took the bowl and left. Piper just gazed at Phoebe, waiting.

I hate when she does that, Phoebe thought.

Piper raised an eyebrow.

"Okay, okay," Phoebe said. "Fine. You caught me. I was planning to do a little Samhain magic."

"By yourself?" Piper said.

Phoebe nodded. "Cole is out helping Darryl with one of his cases today," she said. "So I figured I would try a Samhain spell I found in the Book of Shadows."

"Phoebes, you know that could be dangerous," Piper told her. "Magically this is a crazy day. Your spell could intersect with some other magic and go wrong."

"It's just a simple little talk to the dead spell," Phoebe said. "What could go wrong?"

"Isn't this against the rules?" Paige asked. She watched as Piper and Phoebe made a magic circle on the floor of the attic. "I mean, we're not supposed to use magic for personal gain, right?"

"By George, I think she's got it," Phoebe said.

Paige stuck out her tongue at Phoebe. When she'd first come into her powers, Paige hadn't taken her responsibilities seriously. The Charmed Ones' job was to use the Power of Three to protect innocents. Paige had played around a little bit, doing magic spells for her own use. It had led to some pretty disastrous consequences. Now she knew better than to fool around with her craft.

"It *is* mostly against the rules," Piper said. "But Phoebe seems to think she's found a loophole. And you and I are here to make sure nothing goes wrong."

"It's not for personal gain if we're trying to make our magic stronger," Phoebe said. "With stronger magic, we're stronger protectors of the innocent."

Paige wasn't sure that made sense, and to judge by Piper's expression, *she* wasn't convinced either.

"How is summoning the dead going to make our magic

stronger?" Paige asked. "Who are we summoning anyway?"

Piper turned to Phoebe. "Good question," she said.

"An ancestor," Phoebe told them. "One of the other Halliwell witches."

"Like Grams?" Piper asked. "Or Mom?"

"The spell isn't specific," Phoebe said. "We call for one of the witches from our line, but we can't control who answers. I was hoping maybe it would be Prue."

Paige's breath caught in her throat. Prue was Piper's and Phoebe's older sister, who had died in a battle with a demon. Paige knew that no matter how much her sisters loved her, she would never replace Prue in their hearts. Paige often felt that she was letting Phoebe and Piper down because she wasn't as powerful a witch as Prue had been. At least not yet.

But what if we really can summon up Prue's spirit? she thought. *Maybe she could teach me some of her magic, help me be a stronger witch.* Even though she'd never met Prue, Paige felt a connection with her. They were half sisters after all, and Piper and Phoebe had talked so much about Prue that Paige felt she knew her.

Her excitement faded when she noticed Piper's face. She'd grown pale, and her eyes were sad. "I don't think that will happen," Piper said simply. She gave Phoebe a sympathetic smile. "Don't get your hopes up, okay?"

Phoebe nodded. "I know it's a long shot."

Paige wished she knew how to comfort her sisters. She knew they'd never really get over losing Prue. She understood how difficult it was to lose a loved one because her adoptive parents had been killed in a car crash when she was still a teenager. "Well, whoever comes will be welcome," she said, trying to sound cheerful. She took the box of matches from the windowsill and began lighting the white candles that made the magic circle.

"Right," Piper said.

Phoebe stepped inside the magic circle and held out her hands to Piper and Paige. "Let's do it," she said.

Paige took her sisters' hands. A chill ran up her spine. This was her first Halloween as a witch, and it looked as if it were going to be a fun one!

Phoebe closed her eyes and concentrated on the spell. Her sisters' voices mingled with hers:

Halliwell witches, hear us three.
Into your world now let us see.
On Samhain the veil is thin.
Pull it back and let us in.

Phoebe pictured the veil between the world of the living and the world of the dead. In her mind's eye, she saw a thin, shimmering curtain. Everything on her side of it was crystal clear, but on the other side of the curtain, things looked blurry. She could see shapes moving but couldn't quite make out what they were. "Pull it back and let us in," she murmured again.

Suddenly one blurry shape grew clear. It was the silhouette of a woman. Phoebe felt her heart thumping hard. Could it possibly be Prue? Or if not, maybe she'd get to talk to her mother tonight, or Grams! The woman's shape drew closer to the shimmering curtain. "Phoebe," her voice whispered.

Phoebe stepped back in surprise, letting go of her sisters' hands. She opened her eyes and gasped. The shimmering curtain was real! It was right there in front of her, and so was the woman on the other side. Phoebe still couldn't make out her face, but she could tell that the woman was holding out a hand.

"Phoebe," she whispered again. Her hand stretched into the shimmering curtain, reaching for Phoebe.

"I'm here," Phoebe murmured. She held out her hand toward the woman. When she touched the shimmering curtain, Phoebe's hand felt cold, as if she'd plunged it into a bucket of ice water. Instinctively she pulled back. But at that moment the woman's hand caught hers.

For one brief moment the curtain seemed to disappear. Phoebe found herself staring into the green eyes of a beautiful blond woman with pale, creamy skin. Then the woman vanished, and Phoebe felt a tingling sensation rush up her arm from where the woman's hand had been. The tingling surged through her body, filling every inch of her.

"Phoebe." This time the whispering voice was inside her head.

"Aah!" Phoebe jumped back, stepping out of the magic circle. The candles went out all at once, and the shimmering curtain disappeared.

"Phoebes? You okay?" Piper asked, concerned.

Phoebe shook her head, trying to clear her thoughts. "I'm not sure."

"What happened?" Paige asked, a big grin on her face. "That was spooky!"

"I did it!" another voice cried triumphantly. Once again Phoebe heard the voice inside her head. *"I'm in the world of the living! I'm free!"*

"Do you guys hear that?" Phoebe asked.

"Hear what?" Piper replied.

"A voice. A woman talking," Phoebe said.

"Nope," Paige answered. "But I did feel some strong magic during that spell. Do you think we really made it through the veil between the worlds?"

Phoebe stared at her younger sister. Hadn't Paige noticed the shimmering curtain and the blond woman? "What exactly did you guys see?" she asked.

"Not much." Piper shrugged. "I felt strong magic too, but then you let go of our hands, and the spell ended."

"Yeah, why did you do that?" Paige asked. "I think it was working."

"So you—you didn't see a curtain or people moving around behind it?" Phoebe whispered.

"No," Piper said.

Paige shook her head. "Now you're just trying to scare us with ghost stories."

The doorbell rang downstairs. "More trick-or-treaters," Piper said. "I'll get it." She hurried toward the staircase. Paige followed.

But Phoebe stayed behind. Something was not right.

The servant knocked on the Master's door, hoping he would be in a good mood. When the Master was in a bad mood, those who served him tended to be killed. And the Master had specifically told them to leave him alone today.

The stone door swung open. The Master's giant body blocked all light from behind. His shadow loomed over the servant. "You disturb my slumber!" the Master roared. He lifted his ironclad hand to strike.

"Something's happened, Master," the servant cried, throwing himself to the ground. "I knew you would want to be told immediately."

The Master hesitated, hand still in the air. "What is it?" he demanded.

"It's the witch," the servant said hastily. "Her pendant has become active. It glows, Master. It glows with power."

Now the Master dropped his hand. "How can that be?" he murmured, almost to himself. "Her magic should be gone, vanished from the world."

"S-Samhain, Master?" the servant ventured to say.

"Yes!" the Master bellowed. "There is magic afoot. Someone has opened a portal." Instantly the Master sprang into action. The servant rushed to keep up as the Master descended into the pit below his lair. In the pit, on the stone altar, lay the witch's pendant, a simple cameo, glowing with white light.

The Master scooped up the pendant and held it aloft between his razor-sharp claws. "At last I shall have them," he said triumphantly. "The witch and her demon lover. I shall have them both!"

Piper was just closing the door behind a group of ten-year-old ballerinas when her husband orbed in.

"Leo!" she said happily, kissing him.

"What's wrong?" he asked, his blue eyes worried.

"Does something have to be wrong for me to kiss my husband?" Piper asked.

"I felt a . . . I don't know, a disturbance coming from you guys," Leo answered. "It was the strangest sensation. I can't really describe it."

Piper frowned. Leo was the Charmed Ones' Whitelighter, sort of like their guardian angel. He could always feel when they were in trouble; that way he could orb in to help whenever they needed it. Of course he had a lot of other charges too. Still, Piper knew she and her sisters were always on his mind. But it was odd that Leo couldn't explain exactly what he'd felt from them.

"We did do a spell a few minutes ago," she said. "But it didn't work."

"What kind of spell?"

"We tried to summon a Halliwell witch from the dead. Phoebe felt like having a little chat," Paige said, coming down the stairs, "its being Samhain and all."

Leo's expression was serious. "It's not good to open portals between worlds, especially on Samhain," he told them. "You never know who's going to come through."

Piper knew he was right, but she felt the need to defend her sister. "Phoebe was hoping to get a glimpse of Prue," she said.

"Besides, all three of us were there," Paige told him. "If a demon had tried to take advantage of our spell to claw its way out of the world of the dead, we would've kicked its butt right back through."

Piper smiled, but Leo still looked worried. "You're sure it didn't work?"

"Pretty sure," she said. "Phoebe let go of our hands, and the spell faltered."

"It was kind of creepy, though," Paige said. "The candles all blew out. It was like a séance or something."

"It *was* a séance," Leo told her sternly. "You were trying to summon the dead."

Piper could tell he was stressed out. She took his hand and led him into the kitchen. Some of her delicious French onion soup would calm him right down. "It's okay, Leo," she said. "Nothing happened. I promise."

"What just happened?" Phoebe asked herself. She glanced around the attic. All the candles in the magic circle were out, and there wasn't a trace of magic in the air. But she knew something big had just gone down. She could still feel a tingling in her body.

"*Phoebe . . . ,*" the woman's voice whispered in her head.

"That's it!" Phoebe said. She ran down the stairs and headed for her bedroom.

She threw herself onto her bed and took a deep breath. She was spooking herself, but soon Cole would be home and they would have a nice romantic dinner. She would forget all about the strange sensations she'd felt in the attic.

"*Talk to me, Phoebe,*" the voice in her head said.

Phoebe bolted upright. "I'm losing my mind," she murmured.

"*Look in the mirror.*"

"O-kay," Phoebe said. She stood up and walked over to the mirror above her dresser. She was almost afraid of what she'd see. But it was just her own reflection. A little paler than usual, but still just her.

"*Phoebe. . . .*" The mirror shimmered, and Phoebe's reflection wavered. When the shimmering stopped, she found herself looking into the green eyes of the blond woman from the attic. She was beautiful, her hair piled on top of her head in an intricate updo, her full-skirted gown made of velvet the same color as her eyes. It was no Halloween costume, though; Phoebe could tell the dress was authentic. And very, very old.

"Whoa!" Phoebe cried. "What's going on?"

"*Don't be frightened,*" the blond woman said.

"Why not?" Phoebe demanded. "Who are you?"

"*Pamela Bousquet,*" the woman replied. "*I am your ancestor. You called for me.*"

Phoebe's jaw dropped. This woman was one of the Halliwell witches? But what was she doing in Phoebe's mirror? "Where are you?" she asked.

"*Inside your body,*" Pamela said casually.

"What?" Phoebe cried. She glanced down at herself. Everything looked normal, although she still felt a little tingly. But when she raised her eyes to the mirror again, she saw Pamela gazing back at her.

"*You called for one of the Halliwell witches,*" Pamela said. "*You created an opening for me, and I used it to jump into your body.*"

Phoebe couldn't believe it. This woman seemed to think it was the most normal thing in the world to jump into someone else's body.

"I didn't want to cohabitate," Phoebe said. "I just wanted to talk!"

Now Pamela looked a little ashamed of herself. "*I know,*" she said. "*I took advantage of the day to leap through the veil separating us.*"

"Samhain," Phoebe said, "the day when the barrier between worlds is thinnest."

"*Your spell allowed my spirit to gain access to you,*" Pamela said. "*And because the barrier is so thin today, I was able to force my way through. I could not take physical form, but I could possess your body.*"

Phoebe felt a wave of fear. She was possessed?

"*I could take control of your body and use it to do whatever I like,*" Pamela said. "*But I'd rather have your cooperation. I'm not a bad witch. I'm just desperate.*"

Phoebe studied the beautiful face in the mirror. Pamela's lovely eyes were troubled, and her jaw was clenched. She did seem desperate, and she was an ancestor. *Maybe I should help her,* Phoebe thought.

"What kind of cooperation?" she asked.

"*I must find someone,*" Pamela said urgently. "*Find him and release him from a spell.*"

"Who are you looking for?" Phoebe asked.

"*My husband,*" Pamela replied. "*He's a demon.*"

"Hi, Cole," Paige said as Phoebe's ex-demon fiancé entered the kitchen. Paige had gotten used to the fact that she was the biological daughter of a witch and a Whitelighter. She'd even gotten used to living with two sisters she never knew she had, not to mention her Whitelighter brother-in-law. But the one thing she wasn't used to was knowing that Phoebe's husband-to-be had once been one of the most evil demons to walk the earth.

"Hey, Paige," Cole said brightly, giving her a little fake punch on the arm. "Happy Halloween." He rummaged in the candy bowl and pulled out a lollipop.

"Don't you mean Samhain?" she asked. "We've been having all sorts of spooky Samhain fun."

Cole's eyes darkened. "What do you mean?"

"Well, your honey wanted to speak to the dead, so we did a spell to call up one of our ancestors."

"Did it work?" Cole asked anxiously.

"Not unless one of the Halliwell witches thinks blowing out a bunch of candles is an appropriate way to say hi to her descendants," Paige said. "It was a total bust. I think Phoebe might be bummed about it."

"Why?"

"She just looked sort of weird afterward," Paige said. "So be extra-nice to her."

"Thanks," he said, heading for the stairs.

Paige watched him go with a sigh. Sometimes she relished her single-girl status. But other times she thought it would be nice to have a guy around, especially since both her sisters were so coupled up. *If I had a boyfriend, I wouldn't be stuck on trick-or-treat duty all alone,* she thought ruefully. Piper and Leo had disappeared upstairs after their dinner, and Phoebe hadn't come down since they did the spell in the attic.

That left Paige by herself in the kitchen with a giant bowl of goodies. She eyed the candy hungrily. "Actually, maybe this isn't so bad after all," she murmured, reaching for some jelly beans.

Phoebe was still staring at Pamela in the mirror when Cole came into the bedroom. He slipped his arms around Phoebe's waist and nuzzled her neck.

Phoebe jerked away from him and slapped him in the face.

"Hey!" yelled Cole.

"Hey!" Phoebe yelled at the same time. "What just happened?"

"Sorry. I must've taken over our body for a moment," Pamela's voice said to Phoebe. *"I am a married woman, you know. I'm not used to strange men hugging me."*

"That's no excuse for hitting my fiancé with my own hand," Phoebe muttered.

"Um, Phoebes?" Cole said. "Who are you talking to? And why did you slap me?"

Phoebe looked at Cole's baffled face. This wasn't going to be easy to explain.

"Phoebe, we have to go," Pamela told her. *"I have only this one night, and we have a lot to do."*

"What do you mean, you only have one night?" Phoebe asked. "You didn't tell me that!"

"Phoebe, what's going on?" Cole sounded really worried now. But so did Pamela. Phoebe felt as if her head might explode at any second.

"Okay, everyone stop talking," she said. In the oh-so-welcome silence, Phoebe dragged her full-length standing mirror over next to the bed. Then she ordered Cole to sit in the chair facing the mirror, and she perched on the bed. "Cole, look in the mirror."

He did. "What am I looking for?" he asked.

Phoebe glanced at her reflection—and saw herself. "Pamela!" she yelled. "Show yourself again."

The glass in the mirror shimmered. Then Pamela appeared in the place of Phoebe's reflection.

"Okay, who's that and how did she get in our mirror?" Cole asked.

"Her name is Pamela," Phoebe said. "She's one of my ancestors."

"I knew it!" Cole said. "That spell you did with your sisters—it worked."

"Sort of," Phoebe replied. "We summoned Pamela just to talk, but she jumped into my body instead."

"*I had an emergency.*" This time, when Pamela spoke, Phoebe heard the words in her head, and she also heard them coming out of her own mouth. "*I need to save my husband. There are evil forces after him.*"

"Wait a minute," Cole said. "If you're one of Phoebe's ancestors, and we haven't heard of you before, that must mean that you lived quite a while ago."

"*Yes,*" Pamela told them. "*I died during the French Revolution.*"

"That explains my new French accent," Phoebe muttered.

"If you've been dead that long, then how is your husband still alive?" Cole asked.

"He's a demon," Phoebe told him. "We were just getting to that part when you walked in."

"A demon!" Cole said, surprised.

"*Like you were,*" Pamela snapped. "*I know all about you, Belthazor.*"

Cole bristled. Phoebe leaped up. "Stop!" she cried. "I don't need you two fighting. This is already confusing enough. Pamela, Belthazor was vanquished. Cole is human now. And Cole, I loved you when you were half demon. You should be more understanding."

"You're right." Cole sat back down. "So let's hear this story. You were married to a demon, and he's still alive."

"*Yes,*" Pamela said. "*His name is Qalmor. He was born almost three thousand years ago. For centuries he hunted witches. One touch of his hand would cause his enemy to feel paralyzed. Then he would steal her powers—by draining her life force.*"

"You mean by killing her," Phoebe said, her voice shaking.

"*Yes. By the time I met him, he had the powers of many witches. He was too strong to fight.*"

"So why didn't he kill you and take your powers?" Cole asked.

Pamela bit her lip. "*He—he fell in love with me. After that he didn't want to take my powers. We were married for ten years. When I was killed, he went into hiding. He's never used his powers or killed another witch in all the years since then.*"

"So he was reformed by his love for you," Phoebe said, gazing at Cole. It was a little like their story.

"*Not exactly,*" Pamela said. "*I knew if he loved me, he wouldn't kill me. He was nearly invincible. To attempt to fight him would have been useless.*"

"So you made him fall in love with you?" Cole asked, giving Phoebe a wry smile. She knew he was thinking of their own relationship.

Phoebe/Pamela nodded. "*I cast a spell on him. A love spell.*"

The servant watched nervously as the Master held the glass bowl in his massive hands. It was the only seeing bowl they had left; the Master had shattered all the others with his claws. If this one broke, the Master's fury would know no bounds. And he would vent his fury on those most easily available . . . like the servant.

Slowly the Master placed the seeing bowl on the altar. Relieved, the servant rushed to fill it with water. He held his hand up for the witch's pendant, making sure that he didn't look the Master in the eye. The Master hated that sort of insubordination. The Master placed the cameo in his hand.

Gently, the servant put the pendant into the seeing bowl. It floated on the surface of the water as the magic began. The servant backed away, covering his ears so he would not hear the words of the spell the Master used to activate the seeing bowl.

Knowing the spell was grounds for execution in the Master's opinion.

The bowl came to life, scenes flashing across the water and reflecting on the glass sides of the bowl. Earth, blue and pristine. Then, closer, North America. Closer still, the Northwest. A city . . . tall buildings, Victorian houses, a musty attic . . .

"I have her!" the Master roared. He pointed one claw into the empty air, and a hole opened in the fabric of space. "Go!" he commanded. "Bring her to me immediately."

The servant leaped through the hole. He would bring the Master his witch. Or he would die.

Piper paced up and down in the living room. "So this Pamela person cast a love spell on a demon because if he loved her, he wouldn't want to kill her and steal her powers."

"Right," said Phoebe.

"And it worked so well that he not only married her but also stayed good for hundreds of years after she died."

"Right," said Cole.

Piper stopped pacing and looked at them. Both Phoebe and Cole were acting as if this were no big deal.

"And Pamela is inside your body right now?" Paige asked from her place on the couch.

"*Oui,*" Phoebe said with someone else's voice.

"Okay, stop that!" Piper cried. "No offense, Pamela, but it freaks me out."

Phoebe shrugged. "Look," she said in her own voice, "we have to figure out where her husband is, fast."

"What's the rush?" asked Leo.

"*I must leave Phoebe's body tonight while the veil between the worlds is still thin,*" Pamela said. "*After tonight I won't be able to get through, back to the world of the dead.*"

"And that would be bad," Piper said. "Okay, I get it. We don't want Phoebe to have to share her body with a dead ancestor for the rest of her life."

"No, thanks," said Phoebe.

"So what's the plan?" Paige asked. All eyes went to Piper.

"Let's see," Piper said. "Pamela, you said something is after your husband. How do you know that?"

"*I have seen it from the other world.*" Pamela replied using Phoebe's voice. "*Qalmor's love for me is so strong that it glows like a beacon through the barrier between us. Although we cannot be together, I have felt his love every day since the day I died.*"

"Wow. I am never gonna get used to that," Paige commented. "Phoebe, you've never sounded so poetic."

"Well, if you can see him even in the world of the dead, you must know where he is," Piper said. "So let's go find him."

Phoebe shook her head. "*It does not work that way,*" Pamela said sadly.

"Phoebe, you talk," Piper said. "I can't keep track otherwise!"

"Okay, in the other world Pamela can feel Qalmor's love, and she can feel the danger to him," Phoebe told them. "But it's not clear. She can't see where he is, and she can't see what's after him. She just knows that the danger is growing and that he's going to be vanquished tonight."

"But if he's dead and she's dead, isn't that good?" Paige asked. "I mean, can't they be together then?"

"No," Leo answered. "When demons are vanquished, they don't go to the world of the dead. If he's vanquished, she won't even be able to feel his love anymore. They'll be separated forever."

"Why does she even care?" Piper asked. "His love is false. It's because of a spell."

Pamela/Phoebe looked sadly down at her hands. "*His love is false, yes,*" she murmured. "*But mine is real. Once I had put the spell on him, he was devoted to me. I couldn't help it. . . . I fell in love with him."*

"That's so sweet," Paige said, shooting Phoebe/Pamela a sympathetic look.

Piper rolled her eyes. "Am I the only one who remembers that we're talking about a demon here?" she said. "And a witch-hunting demon too. So why should we save him?"

"He's been reformed," Cole said. "For more than two hundred years, he's been good."

"Not really good," Piper replied. "More like . . . neutered." She knew that this was a touchy subject for Cole because he had reformed himself. But it just wasn't the same situation. "Cole, this guy is still a demon. The only reason he hasn't gone back to his old habits is that he's been under a spell." She turned to Phoebe. "Nice spell, by the way—How'd you get it to last this long?"

Phoebe looked down at her hands. *"I found a way to leave my powers behind after I died, so that my love spell would continue to bind Qalmor,"* Pamela said. *"But as long as he still feels love, he will want to be good for my sake. That means he will not use his stolen powers. He is helpless in the face of attack."*

"That only seems fair," Leo said. "He got those powers by killing witches. He shouldn't use them for his own good."

"So he's defenseless," Piper said. "How are you planning to defend him?"

"I am going to release him," Pamela whispered.

For a moment Piper didn't understand what she meant. Then it sank in. "You mean, you're going to undo the love spell?"

Pamela/Phoebe nodded.

Paige jumped up from the couch. "But you said the only thing keeping him good was his love for you! If you undo the spell, he won't love you."

"And he won't be good anymore," Leo said.

"*But he will be able to defend himself,*" Pamela said.

"Yeah, using powers he stole from witches," Piper cried. "And once he goes bad again, we'll have to vanquish him."

"*No witch was ever able to vanquish him before,*" Pamela said. "*He has a great many powers.*"

"Because he killed a great many witches," Leo said. "And now you want to release him to kill again. How can you do that?"

Phoebe's eyes flashed with anger, and Piper took a step back. She'd never seen her sister look that way before. Maybe Pamela's emotions were starting to effect Phoebe.

"*Don't you understand?*" Pamela said. "*I have to save my husband, no matter what the consequences.*"

"He kills witches," Paige cried.

"*That is not my problem,*" Pamela replied coldly.

Piper caught her breath. Pamela might be their ancestor, but she didn't seem to share their feelings about right and wrong, at least not when it came to her husband.

Phoebe moaned. Cole slipped his arm around her shoulders. "Are you all right?" he asked. She shook her head hard but didn't say anything. "Phoebe? Pamela? Anybody?"

"We need to get Pamela out of Phoebe," Leo said, taking Piper's hand. "Now."

"You're right," she said. The sooner Pamela was back in the world of the dead, the less mischief she could do. She turned to her sister. "Phoebe, let's go up to the attic."

But Phoebe was gone.

"Stop!" Phoebe yelled. "Pamela, stop!"

It was useless. Her body was running down the street, and she had nothing to say about it. Pamela wasn't even answering her. *Okay, I have to calm down,* she thought. *Once I'm calm, I can figure out how to solve this problem.* Phoebe tried to take a few deep breaths. But she couldn't. Pamela was in control of everything, even the breathing.

Phoebe concentrated on watching where they were going. She couldn't turn her head or even make her eyes glance to the left or the right. But she tried to remember everything they passed, in case she could get control of herself later and make her way back.

The last thing she remembered was sitting on the couch in the living room with Cole's arm around her. Then everything had gone black. When she woke up, she was running down the street in a part of town she'd never seen before. Or rather, *Pamela* was running down the street. Phoebe was just along for the ride.

Her footsteps slowed as she turned down a small, dark side street. She caught sight of a neon sign over a metal door. The neon was shaped like an eye.

"Pamela, talk to me," Phoebe said. "Tell me where we are!"

But Pamela ignored her. She pushed open the metal door and stepped into a tiny room. One bare lightbulb hung from the ceiling. An ancient woman with a shawl over her head sat on a big ugly cushion in the center of the room.

"Are we at a fortune-teller's?" Phoebe asked. "Is she at least a witch or just a quack?" The woman raised an eyebrow and looked at Phoebe as if she'd heard her. "No offense," Phoebe added, just in case.

The old lady beckoned for her to sit down, and Pamela lowered Phoebe's body onto the floor. She stared right into the fortune-teller's eyes. Phoebe gasped as the old woman looked at her. She had a feeling the woman could see not only Pamela but Phoebe as well.

"You are too complicated," the woman said. "I dare not tell this fortune."

"Fine. But please help me. I need a crystal and a place to scry," Pamela said. "I'm looking for my husband." She dug around in Phoebe's bag and pulled out a ten-dollar bill.

"Hey!" Phoebe cried. "That's my money! When did you have time to stop and grab my purse?"

Pamela still ignored her. But the old woman lifted her eyebrows.

"Can you hear me?" Phoebe called to her. "Help!"

The old woman snatched the money from Pamela and pulled a crystal from a fold in her robe. "Scry for your demon husband," she said. "But make it quick."

"What do we do?" Cole roared.

Paige bit her lip. She'd never seen him so upset. Not that she blamed him. One minute Phoebe was sitting on the couch; the next minute she'd vanished into thin air.

"What happened to her?" Cole demanded, turning on Leo.

"Quiet!" Leo said. "I'm trying to sense her."

"How could she have just disappeared like that?" Paige asked Piper, keeping her voice down.

"I don't know," Piper replied. "My guess is that Pamela had the power of invisibility when she was alive, and she used it to make Phoebe vanish."

"Is that possible?" Paige asked. "To have powers even after you're dead?"

"Samhain," Cole muttered. "Even if she wouldn't normally have powers in someone else's body, anything is possible tonight."

"Well, that's just peachy," Paige muttered. "How are we supposed to get anything done when everybody's magic is unpredictable?"

"It's more than that," Piper put in. "Pamela said she found a way to leave her magic behind, remember? So that the love spell would continue after her death. I think she still has her powers."

"How?" Paige asked.

Piper shrugged. "We'll have to find her and ask her."

"I can't feel her," Leo said, frustration in his voice. "Pamela's presence must be blocking me from feeling Phoebe."

Cole let out a wordless cry and punched his fist into the wall. "She's going to take Phoebe to her demon husband and release him from his love spell," Cole growled. "And what do you think he'll do? He'll kill Phoebe and steal her powers."

"We don't know that," Paige said, trying to comfort him. "Maybe this Qalmor guy really is reformed. You did it."

"Even Pamela said the only thing controlling him was her love spell," Cole said. "We've got to find her."

Paige felt a rush of sympathy for him. "Okay, so let's think about this. Pamela took off with Phoebe's body. Where would she go?"

"To find Qalmor," Piper said.

"So if we find Qalmor, we'll find Phoebe," Paige said.

"We'd better get there before she does," Cole said grimly.

"How do we find him?" Paige asked Piper.

"We scry for him," Piper said. "Go grab a crystal."

Before Paige could answer, there was a loud crash from upstairs, followed by a wail that sounded almost like an animal. Instantly all four of them ran for the stairs. "It's in Phoebe's room," cried Cole, leading the way.

Paige ran into Phoebe's room and stopped, breathing hard. The room had been trashed, with furniture knocked over and clothes and papers strewn about the floor. In the corner stood a dark green demon wearing a black hood. The demon wasn't paying any attention to them; it was covering its eyes and wailing. "Freeze him," Paige told Piper.

Piper held up her hand, and the demon froze in place.

"What is that thing?" Paige asked.

"It's a serving demon," Leo said, studying the demon. "On its own, it's harmless. But its master can endow the servant with his own powers. That's when these guys get dangerous."

Paige looked at the way the demon was hiding its eyes with its hands. "It looks scared," she commented. "Why do you think it was crying?"

"I'd say it didn't find what it was looking for," Piper said. "We're in Phoebe's room. I bet this servant demon was sent to find Phoebe—or should I say Pamela?"

"And when it goes back to its master without her, it will get in trouble," Paige remarked. "Boy, I've been in situations like that. Poor little green guy."

"Paige, he's a demon!" Piper snapped. She raised her hand to explode him.

"Wait!" Paige said. "Maybe I can follow him."

"What do you mean?" Piper asked.

"He has to get back to his master somehow," Paige told her. "Maybe when he goes, I can orb there with him. Then I can find out who's calling the shots and what he wants with Pamela."

"No way," Leo said. "That's too dangerous."

"I'll just take a peek," Paige said. "And then I'll orb right back."

"No," Piper said. "But if we don't send him back, we'll never find out anything." She waved her hand, and the demon unfroze. For the first time, he seemed to notice them. He gasped, then let out another wail.

"He doesn't seem in a hurry to run back to his master," Paige said. "What should we do?"

Piper advanced on the demon. "Scat!" she said. "Go on, scram!"

The demon backed away from her, still blubbering. Suddenly

a hole opened in the wall. "It's a portal of some kind," Leo whispered. Paige peered into the hole. She thought she could make out a dark room with lots of stone and, in the middle, an altar.

The demon jumped into the hole. Paige didn't hesitate. She grabbed hold of his arm and jumped with him. She heard Piper, exasperated and worried, yelling her name. Then the hole vanished behind them, cutting off her sister's voice.

"Sorry, Piper," Paige murmured. "If I get back alive, you can kill me."

"I see him," Pamela said excitedly. The fortune-teller glanced up from across the room but didn't say a word.

Phoebe groaned in frustration. She'd been trying to ruin Pamela's concentration while she scried for Qalmor, but apparently it hadn't worked. Now her crazy ancestor was going to take her straight to a witch-hunting demon.

Pamela stood up and left the fortune-teller's while Phoebe tried to keep her legs from moving. It didn't work. Outside, Pamela moved farther down the darkened street. Phoebe focused all her energy on her feet. *Stop moving,* she told them. *Stop moving.*

They stopped. "I did it!" Phoebe cried triumphantly.

"No, you didn't," Pamela told her. *"I did."*

"Finally! You're answering me," Phoebe said. "Do you have any idea how infuriating it is to be trapped inside your own body and to be ignored on top of it?"

"I'm sorry," Pamela said. *"But I have to help my husband."*

"Why?" Phoebe asked. "He's your enemy. You made him love you only as a way to fight him!"

"I know," said Pamela. *"But once he stopped his evil ways, I grew to love him too."*

"And you're willing to turn him back to his evil ways rather than let him be vanquished?" Phoebe cried. "Even though he'll kill more witches?"

"*Yes.*" Pamela sighed. "*Wouldn't you do the same for Cole?*"

Phoebe hesitated. Would she? If it was a choice between vanquishing Cole forever or turning him back into Belthazor, what would she do? "No," she told Pamela. "Cole would rather be vanquished than return to his evil ways. And it would be my obligation as a Charmed One to vanquish him if he did. Just like my sisters and I will have to vanquish Qalmor if you release him from the spell. You can't save him, Pamela."

Pamela began walking again.

"But maybe you can save yourself," Phoebe said. "Obviously you were a powerful witch when you were alive, and you were good. But right now you're acting . . . kinda evil."

Pamela didn't answer. She just walked faster. Phoebe felt dizzy. The way Pamela walked wasn't the way she did, and she felt off balance. But Phoebe wanted to keep talking. Maybe if Pamela's concentration was split between controlling their body and having a conversation, Phoebe could find a way to take control again.

"So where are we going?" she asked.

"*Just to the end of this alley,*" Pamela replied. "*I shall call to Qalmor, and he will shimmer here to meet me.*"

"I thought he didn't use his powers anymore," Phoebe said.

"*I am hoping he will use them to come to me when I call for him,*" Pamela said.

Phoebe snorted. "Well, *this* should be interesting."

"*I must depend on his love for me,*" Pamela said. She had reached the end of the alley, and it was almost pitch-black. No one was in sight.

"Wait, what are you going to do?" Phoebe asked.

"*I can speak to him, from my mind to his,*" Pamela explained. "*Almost the way I'm speaking to you now. It was one of my powers.*"

"Telepathy, huh?" Phoebe said. At the moment she wished she had a power like that. She could use it to call her sisters. "What other powers do you have?"

"*I can make myself invisible,*" Pamela said. "*How do you think we escaped from your sisters and your fiancé?*"

"I don't know," Phoebe snapped. "I was unconscious at the time."

"*I'm sorry,*" Pamela said. "*When I took control of your body, it must have sent your mind into shock.*"

As they were talking, Phoebe concentrated on moving her fingers. She focused all her energy on taking control of the muscles and bending her fingers as she'd done a million times before. But nothing happened.

"*I must call for him now,*" Pamela said. She closed her eyes.

Great, Phoebe thought. *Now I can't even see.* But then Pamela began calling for Qalmor. Phoebe had never experienced anything like it before. It was as if her entire brain were filled with the image of Qalmor. Phoebe shared Pamela's thoughts, and it felt like watching a movie of Qalmor's life, from his days as a brutal demon to his centuries as a lonely widower pining for his lost wife.

Her eyes opened. Pamela slumped to the ground, exhausted.

"Pamela?" Phoebe said. "You okay?"

"*It has been hundreds of years since I used my powers,*" Pamela said tiredly. "*And now that I'm dead I must channel my powers through the pendant. It's hard work.*"

"Uh, you lost me," Phoebe admitted. "What pendant?"

"*When I was alive, I did a spell to put my powers into a pendant, so my powers would still exist even after my death. During my lifetime I simply wore the pendant around my neck. It was just like having my powers in my body. But I left word for Qalmor to bury me with the pendant when I died.*"

"So you died, but your powers didn't." Phoebe finished her explanation. "Nifty spell."

"*I wanted the love spell to last forever,*" Pamela said. "*But now I am trying to use the powers from a pendant halfway around the world. It is exhausting. . . .* "

Now's my chance, Phoebe thought. Pamela was too tired to stand up. She might be too tired to keep control of Phoebe's body. With all her strength, Phoebe willed her body to move, and it did!

"Okay, crazy ancestor, I've got my body back," she muttered. "And I'm getting out of here!"

Phoebe had only taken two steps when the alley filled with a swirling wind, and Qalmor appeared.

Paige landed in a small, cramped room that looked as if it had been carved out of a volcano. The walls, floor, and ceiling were formed of black stone. The eight-foot-tall demon in the center of the room seemed to be made of stone too. His body was black like the walls, and his hands sported long, ironlike claws. Luckily his back was to her.

"Yikes," Paige whispered. She spotted a wooden crate nearby and ducked behind it. There was no doubt in her mind that this was the Master. The small green demon from Phoebe's room crossed the room and cowered in front of him.

"Worthless!" the Master shouted. "You're lucky the witch is using her power again. It gives you one more chance to save your miserable life." He waved one of his huge hands over a bowl of water on the stone altar, and the bowl began to glow. Paige watched, fascinated, as images flickered on the glass. She gasped when she saw an image of Phoebe, followed by a picture of a neon sign shaped like an eye.

The Master turned on his servant demon. "Find the witch," he said, "and do not fail me again."

He pointed a claw into the air, and another hole opened up. Through it Paige caught a glimpse of a San Francisco street.

"That's my cue," she whispered, and orbed back to the living room at the manor.

Cole was waiting for her. "Well?" he demanded.

"Are you okay?" Leo asked.

"I'm fine," Paige told him. "The Master was busy trying to find Phoebe. Or Pamela. He sent that servant demon after her again."

"Where?" Piper asked.

Paige chewed on her lip. "I'm not exactly sure," she replied. "I saw a neon sign shaped like an eye, but the rest of the place just looked like a regular street."

Leo and Cole exchanged a look. "Madame Skipsha's," they said together.

"Who?" Paige asked.

"She's an old fortune-teller," Cole told her. "She helps demons sometimes."

"She also helps the Elders sometimes," Leo said. "I guess it just depends on the situation."

"What are we waiting for?" Paige asked. "Let's go."

Leo took Piper's hand, Paige grabbed Cole's hand, and they all orbed together.

"Qalmor," Pamela cried with Phoebe's voice, *"my love!"*

Phoebe had to admit, Qalmor was easy on the eyes. He was tall, with dark blond hair and big brown eyes. He didn't look like a demon at all. More like a soap star.

"Pamela?" he asked uncertainly.

Phoebe felt Pamela getting ready to answer, but she was still weak. Phoebe pushed Pamela down with her mind. "No, I'm Phoebe," she told Qalmor. "Pamela's descendant."

"Did you call me?" he asked.

"Well, yes. And no." Phoebe knew she should run and hide from this demon or try to find a way to vanquish him. But now that he was standing in front of her, she wasn't sure she wanted to. When Pamela had called to him, Phoebe had felt all the love they shared. It was hard to hate a demon who could love so truly. *It's a spell,* she reminded herself. *A love spell. It's not his real nature.* But now Phoebe understood how, even knowing it was false, Pamela could be lured by this emotion.

"I don't understand," Qalmor said. "I thought I felt Pamela's mind calling to me. I haven't felt her presence in so long. . . . "

Inside her mind Phoebe could hear Pamela crying. She did her best to ignore it, but the sobs were heartbreaking. "It was Pamela you felt," Phoebe said. "She was using my body to try to find you."

"She is possessing you?" he asked. "But why? Pamela would never take over someone's body without permission. She wouldn't use you that way."

"No offense, pal," Phoebe said. "But you haven't seen her in a couple hundred years. Seems some things about her have changed."

"No. She would do something like that only if she were desperate," Qalmor said.

Phoebe could feel Pamela trying to take control again. All her energy was focused on pushing Phoebe out of the way. "Okay, stop!" Phoebe yelled. Qalmor looked surprised, but Pamela stopped pushing.

"Let me talk to my husband," Pamela pleaded.

"Only if you promise not to take over my body again," Phoebe told her.

"If you let me speak, it will be enough," Pamela said.

Phoebe glanced up at Qalmor. "This is against my better judgment," she said, "but I'll let you speak to Pamela."

Qalmor's eyes lit up, and he stepped eagerly toward Phoebe, as if to hug her.

"Whoa! No touching, bub," Phoebe cried, backing away.

"I'm sorry." Qalmor immediately dropped his arms. "I have not seen my wife in centuries. I am overeager."

Phoebe thought about how it would feel to be separated from Cole for that long. She couldn't imagine how Qalmor could stand the pain. "It's okay," she said, softening. "Just remember, hands off."

Qalmor nodded.

Phoebe let herself relax so that Pamela could speak. *"Qalmor,"* Pamela whispered, *"there isn't time to say all that must be said."*

"My darling," Qalmor cried, "I thought I would never speak to you again!"

"I have come back for only this one night," Pamela told him, *"to warn you. Evil things are hunting you. Tonight they will vanquish you!"*

Qalmor shook his head. "I have been living like a hermit for hundreds of years. Why would anything evil want to hurt me?"

"Maybe it's one of your old enemies," Phoebe said. "From back in your witch-killing demonic days."

"I see Pamela has told you of my past," Qalmor said. "I assure you, you have nothing to fear from me. I am a changed man. My love for my wife taught me to respect witches and to want to be good."

"But there is evil coming for you," Pamela cried. *"I can feel it! You must be ready to defend yourself."*

"I shall fight if someone attacks me," Qalmor said. "But I shall not use magic to defend myself. The powers I possess belong not to me but to the witches I stole them from. I shall never use them again."

"What about your own powers?" Phoebe asked.

"My own powers had only one purpose: to allow me to steal magic from others. If I touched you, you would be unable to move. And I could drain your life force without any resistance."

Phoebe shuddered. He seemed very matter-of-fact about it. "Well, I'm glad you don't do that anymore," she muttered.

"The time grows short," Pamela cried. *"I feel the evil approaching. Qalmor, will you defend yourself?"*

"No, my love," he said. "Not with witches' magic."

"Then I must release you," Pamela told him.

"Oh, no!" Phoebe cried, interrupting her. "You're not doing that. He'll paralyze me and drain me!"

"I have no choice," Pamela said. *"Qalmor—"*

"No!" Phoebe yelled, using her mind to push Pamela down. Pamela fought her, trying to speak, trying to take control of her body. "No," Phoebe said through gritted teeth. But Pamela was a strong witch, and her desperation made her even stronger.

Phoebe glanced up at Qalmor. He was mild-mannered now, but if Pamela released him from the love spell, he would turn into a violent, and angry, demon. She couldn't take that chance.

"Sorry, Pamela," Phoebe said. Then she began to run.

The servant reached for Madame Skipsha's head. Using the Master's power, he could read her thoughts to tell him where the witch had gone. He dared not go back to the Master without the witch. It would mean certain death.

Madame Skipsha raised one finger. The servant's hand stopped as if it had hit a wall.

"Witch!" he grunted, surprised.

"No," Madame Skipsha replied. "I am not a witch. But the likes of you cannot harm me."

"Tell me where the witch is, woman!" the servant roared,

using the Master's voice. "She escaped me once, but she will not escape again!"

Madame Skipsha leaned forward and put her grizzled old face close to his. She stared into his eyes. The servant squirmed, trying to back away from her. But he couldn't move. It was as if she held him snared in a web.

"Your master's powers do not frighten me," she said. "You will not find the witch here. But I shall not stop you from looking for her."

She closed her eyes, and the servant fell backward as if he'd been pushed. She had released him from her binding power. He looked around her tiny room. The witch wasn't here, but she had been. The Master had seen it. The servant turned toward the door. He would search the streets. He had no other choice.

Piper let go of Leo's hand and looked around. They had orbed into a small, dingy room. The four of them could barely fit.

"The Charmed Ones. I've been expecting you," said a creaky voice.

Piper turned to see an old woman standing in the corner. Her face was covered in a thousand wrinkles, but her eyes looked young and alive.

"Madame Skipsha?" Piper said, guessing.

The old woman nodded. "You do not have much time. Your sister isn't in control of her body."

"How do *you* know that?" Paige asked.

Piper studied the woman's face. "You're psychic," she said. "You're a true fortune-teller."

Madame Skipsha smiled. "I am many things. But as it happens, I saw your sister. The other witch was controlling her body, but I could see your sister in her eyes."

"Is she all right?" Cole asked.

Madame Skipsha gazed at him. "She is in danger . . . because of you."

Cole's mouth dropped open in astonishment.

"What?" Piper cried. "What kind of danger?"

"The other witch seeks to save her love. Your sister is sympathetic to this love."

"Because of me," Cole murmured. "She thinks Pamela and Qalmor are just like us."

"But that's not true," Piper said. "You're not a demon anymore. The evil part of you was vanquished. Qalmor's evil is just being kept in check by a spell." She knew Phoebe tended to be emotional and sometimes impulsive, but surely she could see the difference between the two situations. Couldn't she?

"Madame Skipsha, can you see what will happen?" Paige asked.

The old woman shook her head. "It is clouded."

"You said she was here," Leo said. "Where did she go?"

"She scried for her demon. When she found him, she realized that he was too far away. She left."

"Where?" Piper asked. "Where did she go?"

"She was going to call for him," Madame Skipsha replied. "She wanted to be alone."

"We've got to find her," Cole said, yanking open the door.

"There is more," Madame Skipsha said. "A demon."

"You mean Pamela's husband?" Leo asked.

"No, a serving demon," the old woman said. "He was sent here to find her. He left in search of your sister. If he finds her, he will bring her to his master, and she will be killed."

Piper couldn't believe her ears. Madame Skipsha sounded perfectly calm. "You mean, you just let a demon walk out of here when you knew he was after our sister?" she demanded.

Madame Skipsha looked straight into her eyes. Piper caught

her breath. She thought she could see thousands of souls within the old woman's gaze. This was no ordinary fortune-teller!

"You're right," Madame Skipsha murmured as if she had heard Piper's thought. "I am a Fate. I see many things, but I cannot interfere. Sometimes good wins, sometimes evil. It is the balance of the two that matters. My job is to preserve the balance."

"Are you saying that my sister may have to die to preserve the balance?" Piper asked in a trembling voice. Losing one sister had been awful enough; she couldn't stand to lose another.

Madame Skipsha reached out an old, wrinkled hand. She touched Piper's cheek. "I am unable to see the outcome," she replied. "Your sister interfered with Fate by allowing the other witch to come from the world of the dead. Only time will tell how it ends." She looked around at all of them. "You must hurry," she said. "The serving demon will find her soon."

The others rushed from the room, but Piper was reluctant to leave. Madame Skipsha's gaze was almost hypnotic.

"Piper," Leo said, "we have to go." He took her hand and pulled her out the door. When Piper turned to look back, Madame Skipsha's shop was gone.

Phoebe threw open the door of the manor. "You guys!" she called. "Come quick!" She had managed to keep control of her body ever since running away from Qalmor, but Pamela was fighting her every step of the way. "Piper! Paige!" Phoebe yelled.

There was no answer.

"Leo!" she cried.

"*They're not here,*" Pamela told her. "*Besides, your Whitelighter can't hear you. His sense of you is blocked by my presence.*"

"I don't believe you," Phoebe whispered. "Leo can always sense me."

"*Maybe he gets glimpses of you,*" Pamela said. "*But you and I are one now, and he is not my Whitelighter. The images will be confused. Even if he finds you, it won't be in time."*

"I can't let you take charge," Phoebe said. She collapsed onto the couch in the living room and devoted all her energy to keeping control of her own body. It was like fighting a war in her own mind. She knew she was a powerful witch. But Pamela's powers were obviously pretty strong too. Maybe worry for her husband had given her added strength. "You can't release Qalmor from his spell," Phoebe told her. "He'll kill us both and take our powers. He'll try to kill my sisters. How can you do that to us?"

"I am hoping he will be busy defending himself from the evil that hunts him," Pamela said. *"While he is distracted, you can run away."*

Phoebe rolled her eyes. "That's your plan?" she said.

She could feel Pamela's uncertainty. *"I do not know what else to do,"* Pamela said. *"I cannot let him be vanquished. I love him too much."*

"Well, sorry, Great-great-whatever you are. If he's released upon the world, my sisters and I will vanquish him ourselves." As the words left her mouth, Phoebe realized how stupid she was being. She should be looking for a way to vanquish him! At least that way she'd have a fighting chance if he became evil again.

"It won't work," Pamela said. *"I tore out the pages of the Book of Shadows that told of Qalmor. I knew that because of the pendant, my spell would hold him forever. He would always be good. He was not a threat to witches anymore."*

"Whose side are you on?" Phoebe muttered.

"I was a powerful witch," Pamela told her. *"I did a great deal of good in my time."*

"But now you want to turn an evil demon back to his evil ways," Phoebe said.

Suddenly her body sat up. "Hey!" Phoebe cried. She hadn't

moved—or at least not on purpose. Sometime during their conversation Pamela must have taken charge again.

"Since you've taken us away from Qalmor, I'll have to do the release spell from a distance," Pamela said. *"I wanted to see him again while he still loved me. But using my power of . . . what did you call it?"*

"Telepathy," Phoebe said dejectedly.

"Telepathy," Pamela repeated. *"Using that, I can release Qalmor from the spell right here. Right now."*

Paige stood on the corner where Madame Skipsha's shop had been. "This is ridiculous," she said. "We don't even know where to look!"

"Hold on," Leo cried. "I think I can sense Phoebe!"

A rush of hope filled Paige's heart. "Where is she?" Cole demanded.

Leo's face was scrunched up in concentration. "It's hard to tell," he said. "I still can't really feel her the way I normally do. I thought she called for me, but it's not clear."

Paige shot Piper a worried look. "Do you think if we add our power to Leo's, he can tune in better?" she asked.

"You mean, turn ourselves into a giant antenna?" Piper said. "It's worth a try."

The two joined hands. Then they each placed a hand on Leo's arms. Paige closed her eyes and concentrated on sending power Leo's way. She felt energy pour out of her into Leo. Piper's energy joined hers. Through Leo, she felt Phoebe's presence. Her sister was afraid, but mostly she was tired, so very tired. Fighting with her body, trying to keep control. Paige caught a glimpse of Phoebe lying on the couch in the living room at the manor. Phoebe was struggling for control—

Everything went black. Paige opened her eyes and found Leo

and Piper staring back at her. "What happened?" Piper asked. "I saw Phoebe for a second."

"Me too," Paige said. "I could feel what she felt."

"That's how it works," Leo said. "But then we lost her. I think Pamela must have gotten control of her body again."

"Well, at least we know where they are," Paige said.

"Right." Leo grabbed Piper and disappeared in a shower of white light.

Paige turned to Cole and held out her hand. "Let's go get your girl," she said. He took her hand, and she orbed them back to the manor.

When the white light cleared, Paige found herself directly in front of Phoebe. But her sister looked strange; the light in her eyes had changed, and she held herself differently. *Pamela must still be in charge of Phoebe's body,* Paige thought. Then Phoebe threw something at her. It was a glass candy dish from the mantel, and it was heading straight for her nose.

"Whaaa!" Paige cried, and orbed to a different place in the living room.

Now Pamela/Phoebe stood in front of the fireplace, holding her hand toward the fire. *"I'll hurt Phoebe's body if you try to stop me,"* Pamela said.

"Don't you dare!" cried Piper.

"What kind of ancestor are you?" Paige asked. She glanced over at Leo and Cole. Leo looked worried, but Cole's face was a mask of fury.

"How dare you possess the body of another witch?" he spat. "You're no better than your demon husband!"

"I don't care what you say," Pamela said, her voice shaking. *"I'm going to save him."*

Paige wondered if she could knock Pamela down without hurting Phoebe, but she was afraid her sister would accidentally end up in the fire. As long as she was holding Phoebe's body hostage, Pamela had all the power.

Pamela began to speak an incantation.

> *A love for me I created in thee.*
> *But now I wish you to be free.*
> *Forget your love, for it is not true.*
> *From my love spell, I now release you!*

Paige braced herself for a magic wind. She half expected Pamela's demon husband to burst through the front door, ready to exact revenge on all of them.

Instead nothing happened.

Piper, Leo, and Cole looked as confused as Paige felt. Pamela/Phoebe stared around the room, wild-eyed. "Well, that was anticlimactic," Paige said.

"*What happened?*" Pamela cried. "*Why didn't it work?*"

"Are you sure it didn't?" Leo asked.

"*I can still feel Qalmor's love,*" Pamela said. "*His feelings are unchanged. But the incantation should have worked. Only I have the power to release him from the bindings of the love spell. I don't understand!*"

"Perhaps I can explain it to you," a deep voice said from the doorway.

Paige whirled around and felt panic rise in her throat. In the doorway of the manor stood the green serving demon. And behind him stood the Master.

"Who is *that*?" Phoebe asked.

But Pamela clearly wasn't in the mood for talking. She turned and raced for the stairs.

"Hey! Wait!" Phoebe yelled, trying to take control of her legs.

"Don't leave my sisters back there! They're our only protection."

Luckily Piper seemed to have the same idea. She quickly froze the two demons. Then she reached out and grabbed Phoebe's arm, yanking her to a stop. "Where do you think you're going with my sister, sister?" she growled.

Go, Piper! Phoebe cheered silently.

"*Your magic is no match for the Master,*" Pamela hissed. "*Look!*"

Sure enough, the Master was already shaking off Piper's freezing power. With a roar, he broke free. He thumped his servant on the head, and the smaller demon unfroze as well.

"I did not come to trifle with these youngsters," he roared. "I came for you, witch!"

Uh-oh, Phoebe thought. *He's looking at me!*

Pamela began to back away from the Master, and for once Phoebe was in complete agreement with her. Piper raised her hand to explode the Master, and he whirled on her as fast as a snake. He blocked her power, and a vase on the end table exploded instead.

"Leave me!" he bellowed at Piper. "I want only that one!" He pointed one terrifyingly long claw at Phoebe.

"Okay, Pamela, this isn't funny," Phoebe cried, fighting with all her strength to get her body back. "What's going on?"

"*How did you find me?*" Pamela asked the Master.

He reached into his black robe and removed a chain with a cameo pendant. He held it out to her, the pendant dangling from a claw. A strange bubble of green light surrounded the pendant.

Phoebe felt her ancestor's shock wash through her. Pamela's hold on her body grew weak. "What's wrong?" Phoebe asked.

"*Remember what I told you?*" Pamela replied. "*I put all my powers into a pendant so that they would endure beyond my death.*"

"You mean it's *that* pendant? Are you telling me that the big demon is holding all your magic powers in his hand?" Phoebe said.

"Yes," Pamela whispered. "*I'm sorry. I assumed the pendant was buried in Paris with my body.*"

"Your charm has been in my possession since your death," the Master said. "This afternoon it began to hum with energy again. I knew you had returned to the world of the living."

"*How did you get that?*" Pamela whispered.

"Fool!" he roared. "I sent serving demons after it before your body was even cold! I knew your power was bound to it forever. Did you think your spineless husband would keep it safe for you? He fled before me rather than face a fight."

His voice was so loud that the stained glass in the window was rattling.

Phoebe frantically pushed with her mind, trying to get Pamela to give up control of her body. *I need to get to Piper and Paige!* she thought desperately. *It's obviously going to take the Power of Three to get rid of this guy.*

"What do you want?" Paige demanded.

"*He wants to kill Qalmor,*" Pamela said, her voice trembling. "*He is the evil that I felt.*"

"And your pendant led me right to you." The Master cackled. He held up the pendant and swung it in front of Phoebe's eyes. "You can't release your love spell without this," he told her.

"*But I used my other powers,*" Pamela said, confused. "*Invisibility, speaking to others with my mind . . .*"

"Yes, and every time you used power, I was able to track you." The Master sneered. "But now that I have you trapped here, I find that I don't want you to release Qalmor just yet." He ran a claw across the green light around the pendant. "I've put a lock spell on your pendant. No more magic for you."

The fear that shot through Pamela's mind was so intense that for a moment Phoebe felt stunned. But this was her chance. Pamela was off guard. She pushed through the layers of her ancestor's mind, slowly taking control of her body again. She concentrated hard and lifted her hand.

I have to act fast before Pamela gets feisty and takes over again, she thought. "Piper! Paige!" she called. Immediately her sisters ran to her side. They joined hands and turned on the Master.

"Anyone know how to vanquish him?" Paige asked breathlessly.

"Nope," Piper said. "But I'm really tired of this guy." She turned quickly and blew him to pieces. Chunks of steaming hot iron rained down from where he had been.

"Well, that was easy," Paige said.

"Foolish witches," the serving demon hissed. "You've made him angrier."

"What?" Phoebe said.

"The Master cannot be destroyed that way," Pamela whispered in her head.

Phoebe looked at the pile of iron chunks that were the remains of the Master. "He *looks* destroyed," she said.

Suddenly the pile of iron shot upward like a fountain. Piper, Paige, and Phoebe jumped in surprise. The chunks of metal flew around like a tornado, whirling closer and closer together, until they united to form themselves into a demon. The Master was back.

He gave a roar, then launched himself at Phoebe.

She screamed, and she heard Pamela's scream echoing in her mind. The Master grabbed her by the hair and pointed a claw at the air in front of them. Phoebe tried to squirm away from him as a hole opened where he pointed. Through it, she caught a glimpse of a room made from stone.

"No!" Cole attacked the Master. His punch landed on the demon's granitelike jaw. Cole gasped in pain, and the Master laughed. He stepped through the portal, pulling Phoebe with him.

"The Master," Piper muttered under her breath as she flipped through the Book of Shadows. She needed to find a way to vanquish that jerk, and fast. Not only did he have her sister, but it was getting late. When the clock struck midnight, Samhain would be over, and Pamela would be stuck in Phoebe's body for good.

"Can you feel Phoebe?" Cole asked Leo.

Leo nodded. "I think I can feel her whenever Pamela isn't actively trying to block me. Phoebe seems okay. She's still in control of her body."

"I don't get it," Paige said. "What does he want with Pamela? He barely even bothered to fight the rest of us."

Piper stopped flipping when she saw a picture of the Master's ugly rocklike face. "I got him," she said. She read quickly through the description, then looked up at the others. "He's a pretty nasty one. An ancient demon with really strong magic. No one knows how many powers he has."

"Well, he can make space portals and do a good impression of a tornado," Paige said.

"It says here there are only two ways to vanquish the Master." Piper went on. "One is to melt him in lava, so he can't take solid form again."

"Anybody got a spare volcano?" Leo asked.

"Let me check my closet," Paige said. "What's the other way?"

Piper glanced back down at the Book of Shadows. She could barely believe her eyes. "The other way is to send Qalmor after him."

"What?" Leo, Cole, and Paige were staring at her as if she were crazy.

"I'm serious," she said. "Apparently they're mortal enemies. They exist to fight each other. It says here that if one of them ever wins, both will be vanquished."

"That doesn't make any sense," Paige said. "Why would they fight if it could cause both of them to be vanquished?"

"They probably don't know that even the winner is vanquished," Leo said. "Just because witches know it doesn't mean demons do."

"Besides, they're programmed to fight each other," Cole said. "I saw that kind of thing pretty often when I was a demon. Two enemies, all they know how to do is fight each other. It's their nature."

"That's why the Master is so mad at Pamela," Piper said, putting it all together. "Qalmor was his old sparring partner, but Qalmor hasn't been fighting ever since he married Pamela."

"Because of her love spell!" Paige exclaimed. "Qalmor has been in hiding, and the Master wants him to come out and fight."

"So he's using Pamela to lure Qalmor to him. Then he'll attack Qalmor while he's defenseless," Piper said. "If Phoebe weren't in the middle of the whole thing, they could just fight it out, and everyone's problems would be solved."

"Well, Phoebe *is* in the middle of it," Cole said grimly. "So how do we get her out?"

Piper thought for a minute. "I guess we can try to find a binding spell to hold the Master," she said. "Then we can orb him to some lava."

Paige sighed. "This Halloween sucks," she said.

Phoebe sat in a large cage in the room made of stone. The Master had locked her in here and left her with only the green servant demon for company.

"So, Pamela, want to tell me what's going on?" Phoebe asked. She hadn't felt her ancestor's presence for a while—it seemed that Pamela had given up—but even though she didn't like being possessed, it beat being trapped in a demon's lair all alone.

"*When I was alive, Qalmor and the Master were terrorizing witches,*" Pamela said. "*Mostly Qalmor. He'd kill witches and steal their powers, and then the Master would come and challenge him. They'd fight, and half the time the Master would end up winning some of the powers Qalmor had just stolen.*"

"Lovely," Phoebe said.

"*The Master was stronger than Qalmor to begin with. But Qalmor stole so many powers that he became just as strong as the Master.*" Pamela went on. "*I stopped Qalmor's killing with my love spell. Under its influence he also stopped fighting with the Master. He went into hiding. And the Master never forgave me for ruining his favorite enemy.*"

"So all his roaring and yelling are just because he's bored?" Phoebe said. "I'll never understand demons."

"*But don't you see, Phoebe?*" Pamela cried. "*It's all my fault! I jumped into your body because I sensed that Qalmor would be vanquished today by something evil.*"

"The Master," Phoebe said.

"*Right. But the Master would never have known where Qalmor was if I hadn't come back. By trying to save Qalmor, I led his enemy right to him.*"

Phoebe nodded. "Your pendant shows the Master whenever you use magic."

"*Yes. And without it, I can't do the release spell on Qalmor. He will come to save me, and he will be defenseless against the Master.*"

Phoebe thought about it. She knew Pamela was mostly worried about her husband. But Phoebe wasn't sure it would be such a bad thing to let the Master kill Qalmor. At least that way they'd be rid of *one* demon.

"If you can't save Qalmor," Phoebe said, "what will happen then? I mean, the Master cares only about him. If Qalmor's gone, will he let you go?" *Will he let* me *go?* she thought.

"*No,*" Pamela said. "*The Master hates me too. The only reason we're safe right now is that he's using us as bait.*"

"Oh. Then we need to find a way out of here," Phoebe said. She pulled on the bars of the cage. They didn't budge. The walls and ceiling were made of black stone, as if the cage had been carved out of the cave itself.

"Well, my powers aren't going to help us," Phoebe said glumly, "although yours might."

"*I cannot use my powers,*" Pamela told her. "*The Master put a lock spell on my pendant.*"

Phoebe looked at the pendant on the altar, the protective green glow surrounding it. "If only we could reach it," she murmured, "we might be able to break the lock spell."

She felt hope returning to Pamela. "*It should respond to the touch of my hand,*" she said. "*Magically, the pendant is an extension of me.*"

"One problem," Phoebe said. "Your hand isn't here, remember? It's not going to recognize *my* hand."

The green servant demon suddenly leaped up from where he had been slumped on the floor. He stood sniffing the air for a moment like a dog. "Master!" he cried. "Master, it is beginning!" He rushed from the room.

Phoebe didn't like the sound of that. "What's happening?" she asked.

"*Qalmor is coming,*" Pamela told her.

"No, my love," said another voice. A rushing wind filled the room. "Qalmor is here."

"Okay, we've got the binding spell," Piper said. Paige nodded, nervous. She'd never tried to orb with a powerful demon attached to her. What if it didn't work? What if she couldn't find a hot enough volcano? What if he tried to pull her into the fire with him?

She felt a hand on her shoulder and looked up into Leo's kind eyes. "I'll be with you," he told her. "I'll orb when you do, and we'll both be there to push the Master into the lava."

Paige nodded, relieved. "But what about Qalmor?" she asked. "What if he shows up?"

"Then we kill him," Cole said. "He won't use magic to defend himself, so it should be easy."

"But we don't know how to vanquish him," Piper said. "There's nothing about him in the Book of Shadows except what it says on the Master's page."

"Well, we know the Master can vanquish him, and vice versa," Paige said. "Maybe we can let them fight before we get involved."

"No. Phoebe could get caught in the crossfire," Cole said. "If Qalmor won't fight, we can just knock him out and take him back here until we figure it out. As long as he's still under Pamela's love spell, it should be fine."

Paige took a deep breath. They didn't have much of a plan. But they didn't have much time either. There was only a half hour until midnight. "Let's go," she said.

"Qalmor," Phoebe said, "you're in danger."

"And so are you," he replied. He reached for the door of the cage and began fiddling with the lock. Phoebe couldn't believe it. He was a powerful demon, but he couldn't just pull a cage door off its hinges?

"Don't you have some power that will help with that?" she said, frustrated.

"I don't use my stolen powers," Qalmor answered calmly. "My only power is to—"

"I know, I know," Phoebe said. "You touch someone and they're paralyzed. But I think you can use powers you stole from a witch in order to save another witch."

He looked her in the eye. "What does Pamela say? I am guided in all things by her."

Phoebe groaned. Ever since Qalmor got here, Pamela had been pushing against her with her mind, trying to take control again. But she was weak because of the lock spell on her powers. Still, letting her take charge even just to talk could be dangerous.

Loud footsteps echoed in the hallway outside. The Master was coming. Qalmor, unruffled, continued poking and pulling at the lock.

"Fine," Phoebe growled. She relaxed her control over her body just a little so that Pamela could speak.

"My love, please use your strength to let us out," Pamela said quickly.

Qalmor nodded, grasped two of the metal bars, and ripped them from the stone. Then two more. Phoebe leaped out of the cage and grabbed his hand. "Okay, now shimmer us all out of here," she said.

But suddenly she was flying backward through the air as if she'd been thrown. She hit the stone wall with a thud and fell to the ground, the wind knocked out of her.

The Master had arrived.

Qalmor turned to face him.

"Now let us fight," the Master boomed. "I shall vanquish you."

"I'll fight with you," Qalmor replied. "But first let this witch go. She has done nothing to you. If you harm her, you will bring down the wrath of the Charmed Ones."

Phoebe gaped at him. It was easy to see why Pamela was smitten by this demon, love spell or no.

"Do you think I don't know that your wife is possessing her?"

the Master cried. "It is her magic that led me to you tonight!" He lifted the cameo pendant from the altar and held it up, its protective magic bubble still in place.

Qalmor glanced at Phoebe. "Pamela, your pendant?"

"Yes," Pamela cried. *"All my powers are trapped in that pendant. Every spell I've ever done. Destroy it!"*

"No!" Phoebe yelled, mentally pushing Pamela out of the way. If he destroyed the pendant, the love spell would be destroyed with it. Then she'd have *two* giant angry demons to deal with.

Qalmor turned back to the Master. "You've stolen my wife's magic and taken this young witch captive."

"Yes!" the Master crowed. "So fight me!"

Qalmor charged, but the Master sent out a burst of power that set Qalmor's clothes on fire. He threw himself to the ground and rolled furiously until the flames were out.

"Oh, boy," Phoebe murmured, "this is going to be ugly."

"If Qalmor won't use the powers he took from witches, his only hope is to touch the Master and paralyze him," Pamela said. *"But the Master knows that. He will not allow himself to be touched."*

"Not my problem," Phoebe said through gritted teeth.

As the two demons fought, Phoebe crawled toward the door as quietly as she could. She was almost there when the green servant demon stepped in front of her. "Master!" he whined. "The witch is trying to get away."

"Snitch!" Phoebe said. She jumped to her feet and took him out with a kick she had learned from Cole. "Ow," she murmured. That body slam into the wall had left her bruised and sore.

The Master glanced over his shoulder and sent a beam of power shooting from his eyes. Instantly the stone door slammed shut and locked with a snap. Then he returned to his fight.

"Jeez," Phoebe said, "is there anything this guy can't do? How are we gonna get out of here?"

"*He will kill Qalmor,*" Pamela replied. "*He is just toying with him now.*"

"Lady, you need to get your priorities straight," Phoebe muttered. She couldn't help noticing that Pamela was right, though. The Master was fighting Qalmor with magic, but Qalmor wasn't really fighting back. He was just trying to get close enough to the Master to touch him. Qalmor was already horribly beaten up. She felt a twinge of guilt. He had come here to save her, knowing that the Master would kill him. He must really love Pamela a lot.

The room filled with light. Leo and Piper appeared, followed by Paige and Cole. "Finally!" Phoebe cried in relief. She rushed over to hug her fiancé.

The Master roared with fury.

"The binding spell!" Piper cried. She grabbed Phoebe's hand, and Paige took her other hand. The two of them began to speak:

Like a damper to your flame,
Like a rope to tie your hands,
Let your powers be contained
Until you leave these lands.

As they recited the spell, the Master leaped across the room and snatched up Pamela's pendant. The power of their spell hit him, and he staggered backward. Phoebe held her breath. Would it work?

He raised his massive hand and hurled a fireball at them. But it bounced off an invisible wall a foot away from him and shot back into his arm. He bellowed with pain as the fireball hit him, but he was able to stamp it out quickly.

"There you go, power contained," Piper said. "Are you okay?"

Phoebe nodded. "I'm really ready to be alone in my body again," she said. "What's the plan?"

"Leo and I are going to orb the Master to a volcano," Paige said. "It's the only way to vanquish him. You guys will have to deal with Qalmor until we get back."

Phoebe nodded. She felt Pamela's rush of relief as Paige grabbed the Master's arm and prepared to orb. The Master twisted away from her and held up Pamela's pendant in its protective bubble.

"*My powers!*" Pamela cried.

The Master dropped the pendant to the floor and crushed it under his enormous foot.

Phoebe felt as if someone had stabbed her. She collapsed to the floor, pain shooting through her body. Pamela was screaming inside her, crying as her powers were sucked from her and lost forever. Phoebe forced her mind to separate itself from Pamela's. *I'm okay,* she told herself. *It's not my own pain I feel. It's Pamela's.*

"Phoebe!" Cole cried, kneeling beside her. "What's wrong?"

"The pendant," she whispered. "When he destroyed it, he destroyed all of Pamela's magic."

Cole's eyes grew wide. "That means the love spell is broken."

The Master began to laugh. "I have wounded my enemy in the worst possible way!" he cried triumphantly. "Look at the wretch!"

Phoebe couldn't take her eyes off Qalmor. He was staring down at his hands, which were covered in burns from his fight with the Master. "All a lie," he moaned. "It was all a lie."

Inside her mind Phoebe heard Pamela crying. She grasped Cole's hand. "He'll come after Pamela," she whispered. Cole nodded and pulled her to her feet.

But they were too late. Like a lightning bolt striking, Qalmor leaped across the room and grabbed Phoebe by the throat. He pinned her against the wall in one swift movement. Phoebe gasped for breath. She could feel the paralyzing power of Qalmor's touch seeping through her body. She was helpless. The sweet, good-looking guy was gone; in his place was an immensely strong demon with fire in his eyes. His skin thickened to a dark gray scaly hide, and his mouth widened to reveal two rows of razor-sharp fangs.

"Show me Pamela," he growled.

"No!" Piper yelled. She lifted her hand to freeze him, but Qalmor shimmered out of the way, taking Phoebe with him.

"Phoebe!" Paige yelled, trying to orb her sister to her. Qalmor held up his hand, and Paige flew backward against the altar.

"He has all the powers of a hundred witches!" Leo called. "He's using his stolen powers again. We have to get out of here."

Cole ran toward Phoebe, but Qalmor knocked him down with the flick of one wrist. His eyes never left Phoebe's. "Show me Pamela," he repeated.

"Phoebe, let me have control," Pamela told her. *"Maybe I can convince him to just take my spirit and leave you alone."*

Phoebe didn't have much choice. Qalmor's grip on her neck was so tight that she was having trouble breathing. She couldn't move her arms or legs. The edges of her vision had gone black. "Okay," she choked out.

She relaxed her mind, letting Pamela take over. As soon as he felt the change, Qalmor loosened his grip. "You cast a spell on me," he said icily.

"It was the only way I knew to fight you," Pamela told him. Phoebe could feel her ancestor's fear, but Pamela's voice was steady. *"You would have killed me if you hadn't loved me."*

"I was good because of our love," Qalmor said. "I have been

good for centuries because of our love. I have denied my own nature."

"*I know,*" Pamela whispered.

"And it was a lie!" he roared. "A cheap spell! Our entire love was a lie!"

"*No!*" Pamela cried. "*No, my darling. It started with a spell, yes, but I grew to love you. I have loved you all this time. I came back from the dead to save you.*"

"Why should I believe you, witch?" he cried.

"*Because I'm here,*" Pamela said. "*The spell was to make you love me, not to make me love you. I loved you truly. I came here to release you so that you could save yourself. Why would I do that except for love?*"

Over Qalmor's shoulder, Phoebe could see Cole watching. In his eyes she saw his fear for her—and his love for her. As much as she hated to admit it, Phoebe completely understood Pamela's devotion to this fearsome demon.

"*Qalmor, believe me,*" Pamela whispered. "*I love you so much that I would sacrifice your love for me so that you can live. But Phoebe has done nothing to you. Hate me forever, if you like, but don't kill Phoebe.*"

Qalmor stared into her eyes. Phoebe held her breath, trying to read his expression. Would he forgive Pamela? Or would he just kill her?

"Phoebe is a witch, and I kill witches," he said. "Don't you remember?"

"Help!" Paige cried. "The Master's breaking out of the binding spell!"

"We've got to orb him out of here now!" Leo said.

"No," Piper replied. "We don't know how to fight Qalmor by ourselves."

The Master was growling and roaring as he threw himself

against the invisible walls that held him. It was hard to hear anything over the racket.

"There's only one way to vanquish them both," Cole said. "We let one of them kill the other, and they're both vanquished."

Phoebe saw Qalmor, surprised by Cole's words, lift his eyebrows. The Master kept yelling and hurling himself around. Suddenly Qalmor let go of her. Still unable to move her limbs, she fell to the ground. She pulled in a deep breath and felt air rush through her, invigorating her. "How long will I be paralyzed?" she asked Pamela. "I've got to get feeling back so I can fight him."

"No," said Qalmor. "That won't be necessary."

"*Why?*" Pamela asked him.

"Little wife," he said gently, "did you really think a love spell could work for so many years? Even after your death?"

Phoebe felt Pamela's confusion. Was Qalmor just playing with her?

"You loved me truly," he went on. "And now that the spell is gone, I find that I loved you truly as well. You taught me how to be good."

He whirled to face the Master, who was still fighting his bonds. "Release!" Qalmor commanded, and the white glow around the Master vanished.

Phoebe couldn't believe it. He'd let the Master go! Now both powerful demons were free, and she didn't even have control of her body to help her sisters fight. The effects of Qalmor's touch were wearing off, but not fast enough. Paige, Piper, and Leo all were in battle stances, while Cole was holding on to Phoebe. But the Master ignored all of them. He ran straight for Qalmor, expecting him to fight.

Instead Qalmor bowed his head and allowed the Master to attack him.

"He's not fighting back," Pamela cried.

The Master raised his sharp claws and slashed out at his enemy. Qalmor let him. He didn't even try to use his paralyzing touch. "Fight!" the Master yelled. He slashed again, this time catching Qalmor's chest. Qalmor crumpled to the ground, mortally wounded.

"No," Pamela cried. Phoebe forced her still-numb legs to move and walked stiffly over to Qalmor. She relaxed and let Pamela take control of their body to cradle Qalmor's head in her arms. *"Qalmor, why didn't you protect yourself?"* Pamela sobbed.

He gazed up at her. "When I die, the Master will be vanquished," he wheezed. "Your descendants will be safe from us both. That is how it should be."

"How can you say that?" Pamela asked through her tears.

"I am an evil creature and you are good," Qalmor said gently. "We were not meant to be together."

"But I love you," Pamela cried.

"And I love you," Qalmor said. "But now we're paying the price. I have done terrible things, and you almost did a terrible thing tonight. This must end. Good-bye, my darling."

"No!" Pamela sobbed. *"Qalmor!"* But he was dead. His body turned to dirt and crumbled into nothingness in her hands.

"I have destroyed him!" the Master bellowed. "I have finally destroyed my enemy!" Then he exploded in a ball of flame. When the flame died, the Master was gone.

"Well, at least he went out with a bang," Piper commented. "Is everyone okay? Phoebe?"

Phoebe looked up and was surprised to realize that she had control of her body again. "Yeah, I'm okay," she said. "But it's hard to deal with Pamela's pain. She can't stop crying."

"Well, I hate to be insensitive, but we have to get rid of her," Cole said, helping Phoebe to her feet. "It's five to twelve."

"Come on," Leo said. He took hold of Phoebe and Cole and orbed them back to the attic in the manor. Piper and Paige orbed in a second later.

"Quick, light the candles," Paige said, tossing Phoebe a box of matches. "We have to undo the spell we did this afternoon."

Phoebe quickly lit the white candles that made up the magic circle. In her mind she could still hear Pamela's soft sobs. When the circle was complete, they stepped inside it and joined hands. They chanted together:

> *Halliwell witches, hear us three.*
> *Into our world we let her see.*
> *On Samhain the veil is thin.*
> *Pull it back and take her in.*

Once again Phoebe saw the shimmering curtain, but this time she hung on to her sisters' hands. She felt tingling all through her body, and then it centered on her heart. *"Thank you, Phoebe,"* Pamela whispered. The tingling rushed up into her head, centered on her mouth, and then left her body.

On her right, she heard Paige gasp. "There's a woman in the curtain," Paige said. "Is that Pamela?"

Phoebe could just make out Pamela's blond hair and her sad green eyes. "Yes," she said. "She's going back through to the world of the dead." They watched as the form grew more blurry. Finally she disappeared altogether.

They dropped hands, and the shimmering curtain vanished. The attic was silent. "Well, that was some Halloween," Paige said.

The next morning Phoebe awakened to find that Cole had brought her breakfast in bed. She smiled up at him. "What's the occasion?" she asked.

"Just that I'm relieved that you're . . . you, and only you, again," he said.

"Me too," Phoebe told him. "It was pretty weird not being able to move my own hands or feet."

Cole perched on the side of the bed. "Do you think Pamela will be all right?" he asked.

Phoebe thought about it. She had felt the depth of her ancestor's pain, but she knew that Pamela had been happy to discover that Qalmor truly loved her. "Well, she'll miss his love," Phoebe said slowly. "But at least she'll know it was real love while it lasted, not just a spell."

"I've been thinking about Qalmor," Cole said. "He knew that if he sacrificed himself, the Master would be vanquished. He had all his demonic powers back, but he still sacrificed himself for the greater good. I didn't know demons could be good like that."

Phoebe caressed his cheek. "Demons can't. But Qalmor hadn't really been a demon for a long time. When you take the demon out of the man, he can be good. And he can love."

Cole nodded. "He did the right thing at the end."

Phoebe slipped her arms around him and held him tight. "Do you think we'll love each other forever like that?" she asked.

He tilted her head back and looked into her eyes. "Definitely," he said.

Phoebe closed her eyes and let herself bask in Cole's affection. "Day after Samhain," she murmured. "Happy New Year."

Yule

by Emma Harrison

Why can't I just wiggle my nose like Samantha and make the windows all clean? Paige Matthews asked herself, shifting her weight on her very sore knees. She would have to be talking to herself, because she'd been alone at the Halliwell Manor all day long. Piper was busy auditioning acts for the Battle of the Bands she was hosting next week at P3, Phoebe was off at her new Web publishing class, Cole was out doing his "I need to find myself now that I'm no longer a demon" thing, and Leo was with one of his charges, something about helping her reverse a banishment spell she'd cast on her ex. Apparently she'd stranded the poor guy somewhere in Zimbabwe.

And what am I doing while everyone else is out there living life? Paige dropped yet another crumpled paper towel into the sink and grimaced. *I am doing windows.*

Paige's back ached. She'd been kneeling on the countertop for an hour and her kneecaps were sore. She'd spent the morning at the supermarket, battling irritable housewives for the best produce, a few hours over lunch in Chinatown, stocking up on herbs for the potions cabinet, and most of the afternoon running a myriad of errands, mostly for Phoebe and Piper. This witch was wiped.

One more window, she told herself, inching over. *This place will be so clean not even Piper will be able to find a speck of dirt.*

She reached up to spray the cleaner on the glass and the doorbell rang. "Saved by the bell!" Paige said aloud. She moved to uncurl her legs, and her knees protested in pain from being bent for so long. The bell rang again, and she looked toward the living room.

"Ah, screw it," she said, and disappeared in a swirl of twinkling white light. Moments later she appeared in the entryway, standing now, and smiled. It was great to be a Whitelighter.

"Much better," she said, smoothing the front of her T-shirt.

Paige opened the door to find standing in front of her the single hottest man she'd ever seen outside her dreams. He was a little over six feet tall with chocolate brown hair, bright blue eyes, just the right amount of sexy stubble, and a few earrings that put him over the edge from cool to way cool.

Then he smiled, and Paige's heart stopped. *Come to mama.*

"Uh . . . hi," he said, his well-worn leather jacket crinkling as he shifted from foot to foot. "I'm looking for Paige?"

There is *a God!* Paige thought, grinning. "Well, you found her!" she said, raising one arm.

The hot guy blushed. "Oh, sorry," he said with a chuckle. "I thought you were the maid."

Stung, Paige blinked and turned to look at herself in the mirror by the door. She had streaks of dirt at all angles across her sweaty forehead. One limp curl stuck to her cheek from under the hot pink bandanna she'd used to hold her hair back. Her white T-shirt was spotted with dust. All in all, this was not her best look.

Still, where did this guy get off? He wasn't *that* hot.

"Nice," she said sarcastically, crossing her arms over her chest and pursing her lips. "So who are you and why are you looking for me?"

"Oh, I'm Seth," he said, then paused as if she were supposed to get the significance of his name.

"Sorry. Seth?"

"Seth Robbins?" he said. "I'm stage-managing the Battle of the Bands at P3 and—Piper didn't call you to tell you I was coming, did she?" He finished speaking with a small laugh.

"Can't say that she did," Paige replied.

"Well, she's been a little crazed today with the auditions and everything," Seth said. "She asked me to come by and pick up her planner."

Suspicious, Paige narrowed her eyes slightly. It wasn't like Piper not to call before sending some stranger to their doorstep, and Paige had seen enough demons in cute guy clothing to set her radar off. But then her normally responsible sister had been so busy lately distraction had become her number one personality trait. Maybe the guy *was* legit.

"Okay, I'll go look for it. You wait here," Paige told Seth firmly, closing the door in his face before he could protest.

She walked into the solarium where she, Piper, and Phoebe had eaten breakfast together that morning, next to the freshly decorated Christmas tree (which she'd trimmed by herself, thank you very much). Sure enough, Piper's planner was sitting right next to her place at the glass-topped table. She must have left it there in her rush to get to the club.

Paige grabbed the planner and turned around, and her heart instantly flew into her throat. Mr. Maybe Hot was standing right in front of her, and his eyes were no longer bright blue. They were actually pretty much flaming red.

"Ah, jeez," Paige said, rolling her eyes. "Okay, tell me why you're really here—like I don't already know."

"I'm here to take your powers," he growled, the red in his eyes intensifying.

"Yep, pretty much what I figured," Paige said as she backed up slightly.

He whipped a sharp knife out from behind his back and lunged at Paige. Before she even saw him coming, he was practically on top of her. On reflex, Paige threw Piper's leather-backed planner up to shield herself, and the knife plunged right through it. The warlock struggled to pull the knife free again, and Paige threw the whole thing—book and lodged-in blade—at him, then turned to run for the kitchen.

"Warlock potion, warlock potion, warlock potion," Paige mumbled, yanking open the doors to the potion cabinet. There were hundreds of little bottles of premade potions, liquids, and dry ingredients, and she started to fumble through them, her fingers trembling.

"I'm coming for you, witch!" the warlock called out. She could hear him stalking through the living room.

Paige thrust out her hand. "Warlock vanquishing potion!" she shouted. In a swirl of light the potion appeared in her palm. But the next second something breezed by her ear and stuck into the wall next to her head. The warlock's knife. Paige orbed out again, back to the solarium.

"Oooh! A Whitelighter as well!" the warlock called out. "That's two powers for me when I slit your throat."

"Figures. I just cleaned this room," Paige muttered, thinking of the many messy ways in which warlocks and demons had expired in the past. She clutched the potion as the warlock tracked her down again. Brandishing the knife, he circled the table and stood across from her, half shielded by Phoebe's open laptop.

"What's the matter, witch?" the warlock said with a sneer. "Out of ideas?"

"No, actually," Paige said, steeling herself. She didn't have time to worry about the computer. With luck she could aim the bottle just right. She pulled back her arm and hurled the potion. Yes! The warlock was enveloped in a cloud of smoke. Unfortunately, so was the computer. As the warlock screeched and melted and disappeared in a ball of fire, the computer sparked and smoked and basically exploded. Then the Christmas tree caught fire and quickly ignited the curtains.

"Oh, great," Paige said. "Fire extinguisher!" she shouted, opening her hands. The red canister orbed in from the kitchen and appeared in her arms. Paige shot the foam at the Christmas tree. The kickback was powerful, and she squeezed her eyes shut, shielding them from the smoke and flying foam pellets.

Of course both Piper and Phoebe picked that exact moment to walk in the door.

"Paige! What the heck is going on?" Piper shouted.

"You can stop now. I think you've officially killed the tree," Phoebe said, taking the fire extinguisher away from her.

Paige fought to catch her breath as the little white drops of foam settled all over the solarium. The place was a total wreck—impaled planner, mangled computer, singed Christmas tree, and scorch mark on the floor.

"What happened?" Piper asked, shaking some foam from her hands.

"Warlock," Paige said, exhausted.

"Are you okay?" Piper asked, grasping her arm.

"Yeah." Paige pressed her lips together. "Can't say the same for your planner, though," she said, lifting up the expensive leather binder. There was a nice fat hole through the middle, and the cover had been partially torn free.

Piper grimaced and took the book from Paige between two fingers as if it had rabies.

"My computer!" Phoebe wailed. "Paige! What did you do to my baby?"

"I'm sorry!" Paige said, her body temperature rising. "There were a couple of casualties."

"Paige, all my work for class was on there," Phoebe said. "I have to redo it now."

Paige looked at the both of them with their clean hair and their perfect outfits and their relaxed, made-up faces and felt her blood start to boil.

"Well, you're welcome for vanquishing the warlock that Piper sent right to our door!" she said, stalking past them and heading back to the kitchen. She couldn't believe how ungrateful her sisters were being.

At least they could manage a thank you, Paige thought irritably.

"Wait, the warlock *I* sent here?" Piper asked, following her into the kitchen. "What are you talking about?"

"That Seth guy you hired?" Paige said, turning to her sister indignantly. "You really need to brush up on your background checks."

"Seth? I haven't hired anyone named Seth. And I didn't send anyone over here, Paige. You should have known I'd never do that," Piper said.

Piper had her back to her, so Paige scrunched up her face and silently mimicked her older sister. It was childish, but hey, they were treating her like a child, why not act accordingly?

"That's it!" Phoebe said suddenly, stomping into the room. "My computer is completely trashed."

They both looked at her, major accusations in their eyes, and Paige finally cracked. She felt as if something inside her heart had just snapped.

"I can't take this!" she said, throwing up her hands. "All I've done all day is take care of *your* errands and shopped for *your* food and cleaned *your* house and all *you* can do is get mad at me for not reading your mind," she said to Piper. "And all *you* can do is freak over your computer," she added, turning to Phoebe, "which, by the way, might not have gotten trashed if you guys had been home to help me kill the warlock in the first place!"

"Paige, come on, calm down," Phoebe said, her eyes wide. "I'm sorry, but you know we can't be home every second of the day. We've all had to take on demons by ourselves in the past."

"Yeah, but I seem to be doing it *a lot* lately," Paige retorted.

"Okay, okay," Piper said, raising her hands. "Paige, I'm sorry we jumped all over you. If there's one thing we should be used to by now it's random destruction of personal property."

Phoebe took a deep breath and let it out slowly. "This is true. Sorry, Paige."

"Thanks," Paige said. She waited for her muscles to relax, for the pressure in her chest to go away, but it didn't. Even though her sisters were saying all the right things, it somehow wasn't helping her relax.

"You know what, I think I need to get out of here for a while," Paige said, reaching back to rub at a knot in her shoulder.

Piper and Phoebe exchanged a wary look that only served to put Paige even more on edge. She felt as if their opinions, their expectations, her responsibilities were piling up on her all at once.

"Paige—"

"I'm fine," she said, slightly more abruptly than she meant to. "I just . . . need some outside the manor time, you know?" The moment she said it, she got an idea. A very, very good idea. "I'm just going to go let off some steam."

"Okay," Piper said. "Knock yourself out."

"Yeah. Everyone has to do that every once in a while," Phoebe said with a sympathetic smile.

"Thanks. I'll see you guys tomorrow."

Paige forced a smile and headed past Phoebe for the stairs. It was time to do something for herself. She couldn't remember the last time she'd had a massage or painted a landscape or danced around her room to her favorite music. She looked down at her Cinderella outfit and couldn't even remember the last time she'd been *clean.*

This was not the Paige Matthews she knew and loved. This was not the Paige Matthews who knew how to have fun and party. She missed the old Paige, the *pre*-Charmed Paige, the Paige who didn't have powers, and sisters, and a million responsibilities.

She closed the bathroom door behind her and stripped out of her clothes. Her old college friend Sara Baker had been leaving messages for a while now, trying to get Paige to come out with her to some new club. Paige decided it was about time to take her up on the offer.

For one night I'm going to go out and be the old me, she thought, turning on the hot water full blast. *I can go back to being Charmed tomorrow.*

Paige moved to the music, swaying her hips and closing her eyes and losing herself in the driving beat. All around her, clubbers danced and shouted and laughed, but Paige was in her own little world, the one she inhabited when she danced. It was as if she had been transported to another place, a dark, mysterious place where nothing mattered but the music. She felt nothing but the movement of her body. There were no sisters, no demons, no potions to concoct. There was just her and the beat and the darkness. Paige had forgotten how much she loved the darkness.

"I'm wiped!" someone shouted in her ear, ripping her out of her trancelike state. "Let's go get a drink."

Paige opened her eyes to find her friend Sara tugging on her arm. Sara's tan skin glistened with sweat, and her belly-baring top hung precariously off one shoulder. Half her blond hair had fallen free from her ponytail and hung around her face in haphazard chunks.

"Looks like I'm not the only one getting a good workout," Paige said with a smile.

She followed Sara as she wove her way around dozens of gyrating bodies, headed for the bar. Luckily, a couple had just vacated their seats, and Paige and her friend slid onto the empty stools.

"Two bottles of water!" Sara shouted to the bartender.

"Thank you so much for coming out with me tonight," Paige said as the bartender placed the bottles in front of them. "I had to get out of the house before I killed my sisters."

"Trouble in paradise?" Sara asked with a smirk. Paige knew that Sara had felt kind of thrown when Paige had moved into Halliwell Manor. Ever since she'd become a witch, Paige had gradually been letting her friendships slide. It was difficult to be close to people that she couldn't share her Charmed life with. Hanging out with Sara meant editing everything she said and keeping a huge secret, so instead Paige had been avoiding her as well as her other old friends. She hated it, but in a lot of ways it made life easier. The fewer people she spent time with, the fewer people she put in danger.

She and Sara had been closer than close back in Paige's partying days. They'd both tamed themselves a bit since then—thus the water instead of something harder—but Sara still went out every weekend while Paige stayed home with her nose in the Book of Shadows.

"Yeah, well, I just feel like they expect me to do everything around the house just because they're busier than I am," Paige told her, opening her bottle of water. *Including the demon fighting,* she added silently.

She knew on some level that she was being slightly unfair—it wasn't as if Piper and Phoebe were *totally* nonexistent—but she felt how she felt. And she didn't *have* to be fair when she was just griping to Sara, one perk of having friends outside her sisters.

"You're just not used to having sisters yet," Sara said. "I mean, you were an only child for, like, over twenty years. I bet it's weird suddenly having people relying on you."

Paige's brow furrowed, and she leaned into the black leather rim that surrounded the bar. "I don't mind people *relying* on me. I just don't want to be their servant."

"Hey! Forget I said that! No deep thoughts tonight!" Sara said with a laugh. "We're supposed to be partying."

Paige smiled and adjusted the slim straps on her black tank top. She shook her hair back from her face and took a sip from her water bottle, looking around. Gash was the new club Sara had been gushing about, and it had turned out to be the perfect venue for Paige's steam letting. It was double the size of P3 and was just as packed. There were three separate floors playing three different styles of dance music. The walls were painted black with slashes of red silk here and there, lending to the gash motif. There was nothing in the entire warehouse-size club that wasn't black, red, or silver, from the floor tiles to the wineglasses to the red toilet paper in the bathroom.

With her black outfit and her red fingernails, Paige felt right at home.

"I love this place!" Paige shouted to be heard over the music. "How did you find it?"

"Oh, I know the owner from grad school," Sara said, sipping at her water. "His name is Silas, and he's totally cool. He aced all our business classes with his eyes closed. Totally brilliant. He's actually hosting an Up All Night party tomorrow for the longest night of the year. They're gonna lock everyone in until sunrise. It should be a killer."

"That's right, it's the winter solstice," Paige said. "I almost forgot."

With everything that had been going on lately, Paige hadn't had a chance even to broach the subject of celebrating the Yule sabbat with her sisters. Yule was a Wicca holiday that fell on the winter solstice, the shortest day of the year, to celebrate the return of the light that would come as the days began to grow longer. Paige had done a lot of reading up on the subject over the past couple of months and had found out that Yule was such an ancient tradition that some of its rituals had gotten all mixed up with Christmas. Holly, for example, was originally hung on doors because its prickly leaves were believed to ward off evil spirits like trolls and elves, entities that got more mischievous as the dark months dragged on.

Even the Christmas tree apparently originated as a Wicca tradition. People would decorate their houses with evergreens as symbols of health and immortality during the darkest, coldest days of the year. The greens were believed to protect the house's inhabitants from the elements until the sun returned. Sometime around the eleventh century, the Christian religion had appropriated the tree for its own winter solstice holiday, Christmas.

Paige had in fact excitedly shared this interesting tidbit with Phoebe one afternoon, and Phoebe's response had been: "Oh, yeah? That's cool. Have you seen my suede jacket?"

Not quite as psyched as I was, Paige thought wryly.

She had been looking forward to exploring more of the holiday's traditions with her sisters, but she knew neither of them had had a chance to Christmas shop yet, let alone think about buying candles and draperies for the Yule altar.

"You should definitely come tomorrow night," Sara said. "It's gonna be crazy."

"Maybe I will," Paige said, brushing away her disappointment over not celebrating Yule. There was always next year.

"This Silas guy definitely knows how to put together a club," Paige went on, feeling slightly disloyal to Piper. She instantly brushed the negative feelings away. She was not going to feel bad tonight. This was *her* night.

"Do you want to meet him?" Sara asked, raising her eyebrows. "He's here somewhere. Probably lurking back in his office counting his cash."

Paige turned and gazed longingly back at the dance floor. "Maybe some other time," she said, salivating to get back in there. "For now all I want to do is dance."

Just then Melanie and Shira, two other friends Sara had brought along, emerged from the dance floor and grabbed their hands.

"Come on!" Shira shouted. "I *love* this song."

Paige laughed and slid off her stool, letting her friends pull her into the crowd. She couldn't wait to get back out there, close her eyes and lose herself again. Lose herself in the dark.

Paige blinked at the clock next to her bed. It was eleven fifty-nine. She'd been awake for almost an hour but kept giving herself five more minutes before she had to get out of bed. Now it was almost noon, and she couldn't remember the last time she'd stayed in bed past noon. She wasn't about to be *that* pathetic.

She pushed herself up and groaned. Her whole body ached from the roots of her hair down to the nail on her little toe. And she hadn't had a single drink. Apparently she couldn't party the way she used to.

"You'd think battling demons all the time would keep a person in optimum physical shape," she muttered, crawling out of bed. She pulled her hair back with a rubber band and headed downstairs, the coffeemaker beckoning to her. For the moment Paige had no recollection of what she had to do today, but she had a feeling that whatever it was would be made far easier with some high-test java.

She walked into the kitchen, her mouth stretched into a huge yawn, and stopped in her tracks. Piper and Phoebe both were sitting at the table with those looks on their faces, those amused, somewhat scolding looks.

"What are you guys doing here?" Paige asked. The one day she decided to sleep in had to be the one day they were actually around to see it happen.

"We wanted to talk to you," Piper said, following Paige with her eyes as she poured herself a cup of coffee.

"Don't hang out around the house on my account," Paige said with precaffeine grouchiness. "I'm sure you have important people to see and important places to go."

"What is up with you?" Phoebe asked. "You're acting like you're possessed." She and Piper exchanged an alarmed look. "Oh, God, are you possessed?" she asked in all seriousness.

Paige cracked a smile. Leave it to Phoebe unintentionally to break through her defensive walls.

"No, I'm not possessed," she said. She walked around the island in the center of the kitchen and leaned back against it, feeling her shoulders relax slightly. Maybe they could actually have a real two-sided conversation about this—since they were actually *here* and all.

"Phew," Phoebe said. "All we needed was another body-snatching demon on our hands."

"Nope. Just little old me," Paige said.

"Okay, so let's talk about last night," Piper said. "You were more than a little tense."

"I know," Paige said. "Lately I just feel more like your maid than your sister."

"Paige, I know a lot of the day-to-day chores have been falling to you lately, but you are the one who's here most of the time," Piper said. "I don't think you've been asked to do anything un-reasonable."

Instantly Paige's defenses were back up. Why did Piper get to decide what was reasonable and what wasn't? Didn't Paige get a say?

"Oh, no?" she said, standing up straight. "You guys make me do the shopping and the potion making and the vanquishing. You know, when I was living alone, I didn't have to do any of this stuff," she said. "I wasn't a cleaner. *I* can live with a couple of dirty windows!"

"Well . . . sweetie . . . it's not just about you anymore," Phoebe said delicately. "When you lived by yourself, you weren't a witch *or* a sister."

"Those things come with responsibilities," Piper added.

Paige's mouth dropped open. They were both talking to her as if she were a five-year-old. Didn't she know better than anyone the responsibilities that came with having an instant family? Wasn't she the one fulfilling those responsibilities while they traipsed off to hang with rock stars and take cool classes?

"You know, maybe I don't want to *be* a witch anymore." Paige spat out the words, knowing she didn't mean it, but knowing it would sting them the way they'd just stung her. "Or a sister."

She turned and stormed out of the room, cradling her coffee as she went. A huge chunk of her heart was telling her to go back, to apologize, to try again, but the rest of her wanted to keep moving. All she wanted from them was one measly thank-you, a token acknowledgment of everything she'd been doing for them, but they couldn't even do that.

Tramping up the stairs, Paige vowed that she wouldn't come out of her room again until she heard them leave. She recalled Sara's mention of the Up All Night party at Gash that night, and Paige decided she was going to be there with bells on; she didn't care if she woke up feeling like crap again tomorrow.

She was going to show her sisters who was in charge of her life—even if it killed her.

"How cool is this?" Paige said, walking along the buffet tables that lined the back wall at Gash that night. There were trays of hot wings, minipizzas, pasta, quiche, and other hot foods, plus an entire station with cold cuts, salads, and breads of all shapes and sizes. Paige paused in front of an ice-filled tray that held buckets of dressings and spreads. "It's like they have every condiment known to man."

"I know! Silas went all out," Sara told her, her green eyes appearing even wider because of the heavy layer of black eyeliner she was sporting.

Sara had definitely taken the longest-night-of-the-year theme seriously, wearing a long, fitted black dress with a mandarin collar along with a sleek black wig, black lipstick, and black stones in her ears. Paige had gone with a red, gauze, off-the-shoulder top and a tiny black mini.

"You've got to have a lot of food if this many people are gonna be locked in until the sun comes up," Sara said.

Paige followed Sara's gaze out over the crowded dance floor. Gash had definitely done a good job of advertising the event. It seemed that every walk of life was represented, from teenagers who were clearly younger than their fake IDs claimed to older men trying to hide their balding heads under knitted caps and do-rags. The atmosphere was festive almost to the point of frantic. Impromptu mosh pits kept breaking out all over the dance floor, and a few people looked as if they were giving themselves the workouts of their lives.

Suddenly a guy with a pointy goatee and a shaved head burst free from the dance floor, his eyes wild. He tore off his T-shirt and screeched, then started running around the bar in circles.

"What's with that guy?" Paige asked, taking a protective step back as he breezed by her, tongue hanging out.

"Oh, the bouncers will get him," Sara said. "Silas told me that a few people get wacky whenever they have events like this. Maybe sun deprivation really does make people go loco."

"Silas has done this before?" Paige asked. "How? I thought the club just opened."

"Other cities, other years," Sara said, moving away from the buffet table. "Silas has a few clubs. He even has a couple in Europe."

"Wow. I'm impressed," Paige said, noticing that two muscly bouncers had in fact managed to subdue Screamer Boy.

"Well, Silas is impressive," Sara told her, raising one perfect blackened eyebrow. "Wanna meet him?" She gestured over her shoulder, and Paige saw that Sara had led her back toward the club offices.

Paige turned and glanced longingly at the dance floor. After all, she had come here for the lost-in-the-music sensation she loved so much. But Sara seemed to have a serious jones to introduce her to Silas. Maybe she thought they would hit it off. Paige could just see herself jetting off to clubs in New York and Rome, the girlfriend of the successful nightclub magnate.

Besides, she had all night to go astral on the dance floor.

"What the heck," Paige said with a shrug. "You've been gushing about the guy so much I might as well see if he lives up to the hype."

Sara smiled and led Paige through a door marked "Private

Offices" and down a narrow, dimly lit hallway. The music was reduced to a muted, driving beat that shook the thin walls around them. When they reached the end of the hall, Sara knocked on a large, thick black door.

"Enter!"

Sara stepped into the office, and Paige slid in behind her. The room was plushly decorated with thick black carpeting and red velvet chairs. A tall, slim man with slick black hair stood up from behind a glass-topped desk. He was handsome in that angular Calvin Klein–model sort of way, and he oozed sophistication. As he came around the desk to greet them, Paige admired his confident, poised demeanor.

"You must be Paige," he said with a slow, easy smile. His dark eyes took her in, and Paige could tell he liked what he saw as much as she did.

"I've been telling Silas all about you," Sara said giddily.

Paige glanced at her friend and grinned her thanks. This night was getting better already.

"Nice to meet you," Paige said. "You have a pretty kickass club here."

"I'm glad you think so," Silas said smoothly.

Paige felt herself flush slightly under the intensity of his gaze and was surprised. She was not a person who flushed easily, even with her milky white skin.

"Well, why don't you guys get to know each other?" Sara said with a grin. "I'll meet you back out there, Paige!" She winked before quickly slipping out the door.

"Subtle, isn't she?" Paige said.

"Would you like a drink?" Silas asked, moving toward a black lacquer bar against the side wall.

"An ice water would be nice," Paige replied, resisting the urge to fan herself. Silas kept his office a bit warm.

"So . . . Sara tells me your sister is my competition," Silas said as he plinked a few cubes of ice into a glass. "Piper Halliwell? She owns P3, correct?"

"You've done your research," Paige said.

"P3. That's an interesting name for a club. Do you mind if I ask where it comes from?"

"I have two sisters, and all our names start with a *P*," Paige explained. "Three Ps makes P3."

"Three sisters living in San Francisco, three names that begin with *P*," Silas said, holding out the glass of water to Paige. "I believe I've heard of you."

Paige was reaching for the glass as he said this, and she didn't have time to register the significance before her fingers touched his. The instant she made contact with Silas, Paige froze, overcome by a feeling of dread more powerful than anything she'd felt before. Silas's smile widened, and Paige's heart thumped extra-hard in her chest.

Paige pulled her hand away and instinctively backed up a step. The glass fell to the floor, bumping along the carpet and spilling water and ice everywhere. Paige barely noticed. Silas's dark eyes suddenly seemed menacing and cold rather than welcoming and sexy. Something was not right here.

"What do you mean, you've heard of us?" Paige asked.

"You shouldn't be so surprised," he replied. "Your power is renowned in certain circles. The power of the Charmed Ones."

A chill ran over Paige's skin and slammed into her heart. She glanced around the room for a weapon but saw nothing that could be of use against a warlock or a demon or whatever this guy was. She grasped the doorknob, her fight-or-flight reflex telling her it was flight time, but the door was magically absorbed into the wall.

Nice trick. Too bad I don't need doors, Paige thought haughtily.

Silas grabbed her by the arm and spun her around. Paige was just starting to orb when he lifted his hand and waved his fingers one at a time in front of her face, then closed them into a fist.

Paige instantly felt as if someone had encased her in a vat of quick-drying cement. She couldn't move. She could barely breathe. She tried to orb and nothing happened, tried to run and not a single muscle moved. Struggle as she might to twitch a finger or a toe or even move her tongue, there was no response.

Paige strained with all her strength to lift her hand, but no matter how hard she concentrated, no muscle in her body would budge.

Okay, don't panic, Paige told herself. But it was difficult to listen. Having no control over her own body was totally panic-worthy. It was like basic claustrophobia compounded a million times. Paige's heart slammed against her rib cage as fear took over.

Silas grinned at her, then bowed his head and methodically began to chant in some unidentifiable language. All Paige could do was watch. She continued to strain against his magic, but it was no use; she couldn't even blink. Her heart pounded in her chest, pushing her blood faster and faster through her veins. He was going to kill her, she could feel it. And there was nothing she could do to stop him.

Slowly Silas held his hand out in front of Paige's eyes, palm up. To Paige's perplexed surprise, a ball of swirling, twinkling lights appeared above his hand. It looked like an orb, but each twinkling sparkle was a different color, a swirl of pink and turquoise and blue and purple. It was beautiful.

"That's it, just look into the light. All I want you to do is look into the light," Silas told her, his voice low and soothing.

Paige willed her eyes to move, held her breath, and strained to avert her gaze, but it was no use. She had no choice. The light, whatever it was, was directly in her line of vision.

When I get out of this I am so going to vanquish you, Paige thought. Unfortunately, she had a feeling it was an idle threat. There *was* no way out of this. She was trapped—and alone.

Within seconds of staring at the orb, the oddest sensation came over her. She felt her heartbeat start to slow, her fear start to lessen, the little hairs on the back of her neck start to relax. Then, gradually, her brain stopped working overtime. It stopped searching for an escape, stopped thinking of her sisters and how they would never know what happened to her. It stopped almost entirely.

Pretty light, Paige thought, smiling. Her muscles slackened again, and she was able to move.

Silas took the orb and moved it in front of him, smiling down at a bright ball of light that had appeared within the swirling exterior. He pushed the orb toward his chest, and it pressed *through* him, as if his clothing and skin were porous. His head snapped back, and a glowing white light surrounded him as he finished the transfer and the orb was completely sucked into his body.

Paige's legs went out from under her. Silas moved a chair behind her, and she fell into it, feeling completely and totally exhausted, spaced. For a moment Silas leaned back into his desk, catching his breath. When he looked up again, his white skin shone with a healthy glow and his eyes seemed to glitter with excitement. Somehow, he almost looked as if he had grown a little. He stood slightly taller, and his shoulders seemed to have filled out his suit.

"It is done!" Silas called out.

A door in the corner opened. Paige hadn't noticed the door before, but she didn't feel surprised. She didn't feel shocked or disgusted or scared or curious when a huge, hulking demon walked in, his scaly purple skin almost hidden by a hooded black cloak.

"We've done it, Master," Silas said, spreading his arms wide. "We have a Charmed One. She's all ours. I can feel the power of her essence flow through me. Her strength doubles my own." He clenched his hands into fists and looked at them as if fascinated.

The demon smiled, each of its teeth a sharp yellow dagger. "We shall proceed with the plan," it said in a low growl.

"You see, Miss Matthews, you played right into our hands," Silas told Paige, resting his hand over his heart, the place where the orb had disappeared. "As you well know, this solstice is one of the most sacred nights of the year, and it is the only day our ritual can be completed."

He leaned back on the edge of the desk, lacing his fingers together. "We are about to plunge this city into eternal darkness. And once we have the city under control, the darkness will spread—first through this state, then the country, finally the world."

He leaned forward and touched her nose with the tip of his finger. Paige vaguely felt the sensation of his skin on hers, but nothing else. "And because we have you, your precious Charmed Ones will be able to do nothing to stop us."

The Charmed Ones, Paige thought, the words floating through her mind like a balloon through a foggy sky. *That's important somehow. . . .*

But the thought was already gone, enveloped in the mist that seemed to have replaced her brain. She gazed at Silas, not fully recalling who he was, where she was, or why.

A door behind Paige opened, and Sara appeared. "Hey, guys! How's it going in here?" she asked. She paused in the center of the room and looked at Paige. "Hey . . . are you all right?" she asked, her brow furrowing.

When Paige didn't answer Sara turned to Silas. "What's wrong with—"

That was when Sara saw the demon hovering in the corner. She screamed at the top of her lungs, but before she could run, Silas worked his magic on her. She froze, and soon Silas was chanting. A swirling ball of light appeared over his hand.

Huh, she's my friend, Paige thought, the words coming to her ever so slowly. She watched as Sara stared, frozen in place, as Silas once again absorbed the orb into his chest. *I should do something to . . . help her.*

But the thought disappeared more quickly than it came, and Paige found herself staring at an abstract painting on the wall behind Silas, sucked into its swirling hues and shapes as Sara tumbled to the ground.

"Sorry. I'm all out of chairs," Silas said, sneering down at Sara's limp form.

"Your strength *is* growing," the demon stated, sounding pleased.

"It was the Charmed One. With every essence I can feel my power expand, but hers . . ." Silas's voice trailed off, and he closed his eyes as a smile played across his lips. "Soon I shall be able to absorb more than one with each sphere."

"We shall test that theory tonight," the demon replied. "You had better be prepared."

"I shall be," Silas replied, holding his hands over his chest contentedly. "I shall be. Now I should take these ladies back out to the party. After all, it will be their last."

Paige watched as Silas leaned down and helped Sara to her feet. He wrapped one arm around her waist, then pulled Paige out of her chair with his free hand. Together they started back down the long hallway to the club. Somewhere deep inside, Paige heard a voice cry out to fight. To do something. To snap the hell out of it.

But as she emerged into the noisy club, the voice grew faint and within seconds it had disappeared entirely.

Paige, sitting next to Sara on a black velvet couch against the wall, was unaware of the ravers still partying on the dance floor in front of her, unaware of the strobe lights, the pounding music, the laughter and screeches and shouts. She was also unaware that the couches around her were packed with more people just like her, zombielike beings staring off into space, thinking about nothing, caring about nothing. Hours ago they all had been full of life, full of dreams and hopes and emotions. Then they had been introduced to Silas. Now they were just stylishly dressed husks of their former selves.

Throughout the night Silas had been ushering larger and larger groups of people back to his office and returning them to different parts of the club. Each time he returned from his office his spirits seemed to rise. And if Paige had been up to noticing details, she would have seen that he appeared to be growing ever taller, more robust. With each essence he absorbed, Silas was becoming more and more powerful.

Someone dropped into the small space between Paige and the guy next to her, and Paige slowly moved over until the person was no longer sitting on her hand. She took a deep breath and let it out slowly.

This place is strange. Her mind put the words together slowly. *It's not home. I should be home.*

But she didn't have the energy to get up. She didn't have the energy to *care* about the fact that she didn't have the energy to get up. Somewhere, deep in the recesses of her mind, Paige was aware that something was not right. But she didn't care about that either.

A few feet away from the edge of the couch, a group of partyers headed for the door, dragging their feet after a night of nonstop action. It was time for the sun to come up, time for the doors to open, time for the diehards who had agreed to lock themselves in for the longest night of the year to go home and finally crash.

But as they approached the double doors, two massive bouncers stepped in front of the exit, blocking their path.

"Come on, man," a tow-haired teenager said wearily. "Party's over."

"Not time to go yet," one of the beefy bouncers replied.

"Dude! It's seven twenty-two! Sunup! Now get the hell out of the way!" a surfer type shouted from the back of the crowd.

Suddenly the music cut off with a deafening scratch, and the hundreds of people in the club groaned and held their ears, looking around at the DJ. But the DJ was no longer there. In his place was Silas, larger than life, smiling his bloodcurdling smile as he gazed out over the throng.

"Ladies and gentlemen, I have an announcement to make!" Silas called out, raising his arms out at his sides. "You have agreed to be locked in at Gash until the sun comes up. I am here to tell you that the sun is not going to come up. Not now, not ever again."

A mumble of disbelief spread across the crowd. Paige just sat and stared, her attention caught by the rainbow-colored sequins on the skirt of the girl in front of her.

Pretty . . . , Paige thought, smiling slightly.

"And that means, my little friends, that you are not going anywhere." Silas went on, his voice ominous with glee.

He bowed his head and began to chant. When he raised his hands, palms up before the room, a sphere the size of a beach ball appeared in front of him. A few of the spectators stumbled back, but it was no use. Silas's power was too great. Suddenly bright balls of light began to appear within the sphere, and people fell limply to the ground all over the dance floor. A few screamed and cried out, but their misery was cut short as their essences were quickly ripped free. With each essence the sphere absorbed, it pulsed and expanded until it completely camouflaged Silas.

When the transfers were complete, Silas placed his hands on the side of the sphere and compressed it until it was the size of a grapefruit. As he pressed the sphere into his body, his head snapped back and his eyes rolled into his head. A shimmering white light appeared around him, pulsing brighter and brighter. When the huge, hulking demon from his office joined him on-stage, Silas had grown to match his size.

"Well done, my friend," the demon said, bowing to Silas. He looked across the club at the bouncers and raised his chin. "Ask our friends to join us."

Doors on either side of the club opened, and dozens of demons and vampires, some grotesque and deformed, others handsome and humanlike save for fangs, streamed out of the basement and formed a circle on the dance floor. They stepped over prone bodies, looking down at them in disbelief.

"They still breathe," one horned demon said to a vampire as he knelt to touch a young girl at his feet. "They are still warm."

"You see what we can do for you!" the demon called out to the gathered crowd. "They are alive. They are ripe. But they will not fight you. Soon our darkness will envelop the world, the human race will fall at our feet, and we shall inherit the earth!"

The demons cheered, raising their arms in the air. "All hail Nacht!" they called out. "All hail Silas!"

Silas reached his arms up to quiet the crowd. As the demons fell silent, he smiled wickedly. "There will be time enough for that," he said. "For now you will benefit from the fruits of our labor. These people were brought here for you," he said, sweeping his arm to take in the whole room of zombielike clubbers. "Do with them what you please."

The demons whipped into a frenzy, descending upon their helpless victims with savage ferocity as Silas and Nacht sat back and watched, satisfied over a job well done.

"It is only a matter of time now," Silas said. "The Charmed Ones will be powerless. There is nothing anyone can do to stop us."

He smiled across the room at Paige, who sat against the wall and waited, gazing at nothing, waiting to die.

Piper opened her sleep-heavy eyes and looked at the clock, then out window at the pitch-black sky, then back at the clock. Shouldn't the sun have come up and irritated her out of her slumber by now? The wail of a siren split the air, and Piper sat up straight, her Charmed One senses tingling.

Something was very wrong.

"Leo!" she exclaimed, slapping his chest with the back of his hand. "Wake up!"

"What . . . it's not even morning . . . ," Leo said, starting to roll away from her. Sometimes in a half-asleep state he tended to forget that he and his family were involved in a twenty-four-hour kind of lifestyle.

"Piper! There's no sun!" Phoebe called out, bursting into the room in her red silk pajamas, her hair in a high ponytail. She was already clutching the Book of Shadows to her chest. Cole followed her, shoving his arms into a sweater, his hair still mussed from sleep.

"What?" Piper snapped, any leftover grogginess quickly fading.

"It's all over the news," Cole informed them. "The sun didn't come up, and all hell is breaking loose."

"No sun?" Leo asked, waking up fully now.

The four of them turned toward the windows at the sound of a distant scream, and then Leo and Piper jumped out of bed. Piper reached for the clothes she'd thrown on her chair the night before and started to get dressed. Leo pulled on a shirt and looked up toward the ceiling.

"They're calling me," he said.

"Go find out if they know what's going on," Phoebe said, shooing him with one hand.

Leo orbed out in a swirl of light, still buttoning the front of his wrinkled blue shirt, and Piper jumped at the screech of another siren, closer to the manor this time. She still had barely processed what was happening. How could the sun just forget to rise?

"Come on," Phoebe said, reaching out her hand to Piper. "You have to see this."

Hand in hand, the two sisters rushed downstairs, Cole in tow. The TV in the parlor was tuned to the local news. Phoebe dropped onto the couch and started flipping through the Book of Shadows, one eye on the TV while Cole hovered protectively behind her, his arms crossed over his chest. Piper stood in front of the set, her heart pounding, her mouth going dry.

"This is very not good," she said. The harried blond news anchor threw the story to a young reporter, trying to stay on his feet as frightened citizens rushed along the sidewalk behind him.

"A riot has been sparked in Haight-Ashbury and is quickly spreading to neighboring areas," the reporter said, glancing over his shoulder, clearly concerned for his own safety. "The best advice at this time is to stay in your homes, and don't call 911 unless it's a true emergency. Police, EMTs, and firefighters already have their hands full. . . ."

"You guys, this is very not good." Piper repeated herself, turning to her sister, who now sat cross-legged on the couch, glasses on, the Book of Shadows open on her lap. "Could a demon do something like this?" Piper asked, directing her attention to her former demon, soon-to-be brother-in-law.

Cole frowned, two little creases forming above his nose. "Only a seriously powerful upper-level demon could effect change on the solar system like this. Even then all the elements would have to align in exactly the right way."

"But it's not impossible," Piper said.

"Not theoretically, no," Cole told her. "But I can't think of anyone still alive who has that kind of power."

"Phoebe?" Piper prompted.

"I'm working on it," Phoebe replied, scanning the page in front of her. "But so far no mention of the sun failing to rise. Where the heck is Paige? How can she sleep through this?"

"I guess she was out late again," Piper said. "May as well let her sleep until we figure out what we can do."

"We have been kind of hard on her lately," Phoebe commented.

Piper sat down slowly on the edge of the coffee table, her knees feeling weak, and returned her attention to the TV. News vans were stationed throughout the city, covering stories of mayhem and panic that had broken out since the sun had failed to rise at its scheduled time half an hour earlier. Hundreds of people had taken to the streets, watching the sky for any sign of an explanation. Already prophets were popping up all over San Francisco, predicting the end of the world. The poor anchorwoman behind the desk grew more and more flustered, having a hard time keeping track of it all, flipping back and forth from one field reporter to another.

Suddenly Leo orbed into the room in front of Piper, his expression grim. "The Elders aren't sure how this could have happened, but they're working on it. The situation up there is a little . . . chaotic. They sense some serious black magic is involved."

"Ya think?" Piper asked sarcastically. Sometimes the Elders' habit of stating the obvious got on her nerves, especially with her residual resentment over the fact that they'd kept her and Leo apart for so long.

"Well, they're not used to this kind of sneak attack," Leo told her, his brow creasing. "Something about this has everyone spooked."

"The Elders are spooked," Phoebe said, looking up from the book. "That's not something you like to hear."

"I think it's time to wake up Sleeping Beauty," Cole said.

"My thoughts exactly," Piper put in.

Paige was just going to have to put her current anti-Charmed attitude on hold for a while. When the Elders were freaking, it was time for a little Power of Three powwow. Also, Piper was sure that Paige would be ready to work when she heard what was going on. Paige was a good person, and she was dedicated to her destiny. She was just going through the doubting period that every one of them had experienced—more than once.

"I'll go," Leo said, orbing out in a swirl of white light.

"Serious black magic, huh?" Phoebe said, looking up at Cole. "Sounds like you were right."

"I didn't want to be," Cole said, reaching down and kneading Phoebe's shoulder.

"The question is, What would anyone have to gain from making sure the sun don't shine?" Piper asked, her fear heightening with every word.

"Well, that's easy," Cole said with a scoff and a smile. "How many of the creatures you guys have fought either are afraid of sunlight or can't even survive in it? That's why they call them creatures of the night. When I was still Balthazor, I would have been having a field day with—"

Piper and Phoebe both shot him an admonishing glance. Cole snapped his mouth shut and cleared his throat, looking sheepish for a split second. "Sorry."

Piper's heart thumped, and she had to sit down again. "So now these creatures of the night have the run of the city," she said, pushing her hand into her hair.

"It's demon Mardi Gras out there," Phoebe said, glancing toward the window at the sound of a bloodcurdling scream. "And it's only gonna get worse."

Leo orbed back into the room alone. "Paige isn't in her bedroom," he said, sounding worried.

"Great. She must have stayed out all night," Piper said, her hand slapping into her lap. Paige's inner party animal had picked the wrong time to get wild again. "Can you sense her, Leo?" she asked, exasperated. "We kinda need the Power of Three here."

Leo looked off over Piper's head, concentrating. He blinked and then closed his eyes. Piper watched him carefully. "What's wrong?" she asked, her sisterly intuition going on high alert.

"I sense her, but it's very faint. Something's not right," Leo replied.

Piper and Phoebe exchanged an alarmed glance. "Leo," Piper said firmly, "go get her."

Leo had no idea what to expect when he orbed to Paige's side, but he definitely couldn't have predicted the situation that met him. People sat catatonically all around a glittering red dance floor, where demons were attacking limp victims, who weren't even bothering to fight back. Something about the staring eyes and the relative quiet in a room that should have been full of screams caused Leo's vision to blur.

Snap out of it, he told himself, trying to focus. He dropped to his knees over a young girl's body and attempted to heal a wound in her neck, but he was too late. She was already dead. So was the man next to her, and the teenager next to him. Feeling suddenly helpless in the face of so many victims, Leo looked around the cavernlike room for help.

"Paige," he said under his breath.

She was sitting against the wall on a wide velvet bench, her eyes open and staring and her arms limp at her sides. For one long, sickening moment Leo was certain she was dead. Tears of desperation sprang to his eyes as he fell to his knees in front of her and placed his hands over her stomach, feeling for anything he could heal. His palms glowed as he moved them over her body, but there was nothing. Not just nothing broken or torn, not just nothing to heal, there was nothing at all.

A chill shot up Leo's arms, down his back and over his entire body. He could feel that her heart was still beating, that her blood still ran through her veins, but it was as if there were no Paige in Paige. Leo pulled his hands away, startled and suddenly nauseated. He didn't like this—not at all.

Then, to his surprise, Paige blinked.

"Paige?" Leo asked, searching her eyes for a sign of life.

She blinked again, and her eyes moved about weakly as if she were trying to focus. "Leo?" she said.

Then she fell back to staring at some point over his shoulder. Leo's first instinct was to try to heal her again—something was obviously very wrong—but a loud screech got his adrenaline pumping, and he realized there wasn't time. If he wanted to get out of here alive, he was going to have to orb . . . now.

He picked Paige up in his arms, where she hung like a rag doll, and orbed back to the manor.

"Leo! Omigod! Paige!" Piper cried out the moment Leo

appeared in the middle of the parlor. He bent down and laid Paige on the couch. Piper, Phoebe, and Leo all hovered over her, concerned, while Cole kept his distance in the corner. Paige simply gazed past the huddle around her toward the ceiling, an almost content look on her face.

"What's wrong with her?" Cole asked.

Phoebe leaned down and snapped her fingers in front of Paige's eyes a few times. She never even batted an eyelash. "Leo?" Phoebe asked, looking up at him with raised eyebrows.

"Something's wrong," Leo said. "I tried to heal her, but there's nothing to heal."

"So she's not hurt," Piper said.

"No, that's not it," Leo replied, trying to think of a way to put it accurately. "It was like I couldn't connect with her."

"What do you mean, you couldn't connect with her?" Phoebe asked. Her voice grew louder and more tense with every word. "Explain, Leo."

Leo sighed and paced away, searching for the right words. "You know how love is the trigger for my healing?" Leo asked, looking at Piper. They had switched powers once so that Piper could heal him, and she had learned firsthand that she had to pour her heart into it to make it work.

"Yeah," Piper told him, "I recall." It had been only one of the more traumatic experiences of a high-in-trauma life.

"Well, in order to connect with someone that way, you have to touch her soul." His gaze traveled over to Paige's blank face, and he tried not to shudder, recalling what he had felt just now at the club. "But with Paige . . . it was like there was nothing there."

"Are you trying to tell us that our sister's soul is gone?" Phoebe asked softly.

"I don't think so . . . not exactly," Leo said. "She recognized me. I don't know. This is new."

The four of them watched Paige, but there wasn't much to see. Leo could barely even see her chest rising and falling as she breathed. It was as if her body were putting in the most minute effort possible to do the things it needed to do to stay alive.

"There's more," Leo said, swallowing hard. Piper and Phoebe turned to stare at him, their faces grim and wondering. What more could there possibly be? "At the club, it was . . . it was like a demon free-for-all," Leo told them. "There were demons everywhere and they were . . . killing."

Phoebe went ashen and sat down next to Paige's legs. "How many people?" she asked.

"Dozens," Leo replied, trying not to recall the horrifying images he'd seen. "Maybe hundreds. And they all seemed to be in the same state as Paige."

"Hundreds?" Phoebe repeated.

Leo took a deep breath to keep from breaking down at the thought of all those innocent people losing their lives. "I—I wanted to save them, but I had to get Paige out of there. If we'd stayed another second, we both would have been killed."

"What are we going to do?" Piper asked, looking ill.

"It sounds like the club was a setup," Cole said, stepping away from the wall. "Different kinds of demons don't intermingle unless they have good reason to. Someone must have given them a heads-up."

"I agree," Leo said.

"Great. So we go to the club," Piper said, always happy to have a defined task.

"We're not going back there," Leo told her. "You can't fight that many demons without the Power of Three."

"So what, Leo?" Phoebe said. "What do we do?"

Leo took a deep breath, letting Phoebe's accusatory tone roll off his back. He knew she didn't mean to jump all over him. She was just concerned for her sister—and the world.

"Maybe Paige saw something," he said, tilting his head skeptically.

"Leo, she's catatonic," Piper replied, crossing her arms over her chest. "I don't think she's going to be telling us anything anytime soon."

"Well, it's worth a try," Phoebe said. She looked up at Cole. "C'mere. Help me sit her up."

Phoebe stood, and she and Cole each lifted one of Paige's arms and maneuvered her until she was sitting up in the center of the couch. The constant staring was eerie, and Leo found himself looking away every now and again to keep himself from shivering. Piper sat on the coffee table across from Paige, and Phoebe knelt at her feet.

"Paige? Can you hear me?" Phoebe asked loudly.

"Yeah," Paige said lazily. "Stop yelling."

Cole chuckled, and Paige and Piper exchanged a surprised look. Leo felt a surge of hope shoot through him. Maybe they hadn't lost Paige after all. Maybe his plan would work.

"Sweetie, did you see anything weird at the club?" Piper asked. "Do you know who was in charge?"

"Some guy named Silas," Paige responded, leaning her head back into the cushion.

"Silas?" Cole echoed, his eyes widening slightly. "Dark hair, pasty skin, pointy nose?"

"Yeah, that's him," Paige said.

"You know him?" Piper asked.

"Did. Once," Cole replied, his mind clearly working something over. "Keep her talking."

"Do you have any idea what he's trying to do?" Phoebe asked, turning back to Paige. "Did he keep the sun from rising today?"

"Yep," Paige replied. "He and his demon boss worked a spell to bring about eternal darkness, and they figure it's gonna keep growing and growing until it takes over the world."

There was a moment of stunned silence—not only over Paige's revelation but over the detached, bored, dopey way in which she related it. As if she couldn't have cared less and would never have bothered telling them if they hadn't asked her point-blank.

"What did this demon boss look like?" Cole asked.

"Purple skin. Pointed yellow teeth. He was *big*," Paige replied. The first emphasis of the entire conversation was placed on the word *big*. "I need to lie down now."

With that, Paige slumped down into the couch again, resting her head on one of the throw pillows. Luckily this time she closed her eyes, blocking out the freaky stare thing she'd adopted.

"All right, Cole, what do you know about Silas and his purple friend?" Piper asked, standing. "Any idea how they did this to Paige?"

"Silas is a lower-level demon. He was always fascinated with mind control, but he'd only mastered parlor tricks the last time I'd seen him," Cole said, rubbing his chin. "Of course that was about a hundred years ago. He used to try to hypnotize dealers during demon poker games so he could manipulate his hand. Crazy guy." Cole smiled again as if recalling a fond memory, then quickly snapped back to the present. "Sorry . . . again."

Piper sighed. "And the demon?"

"If it's who I think it is, we're in serious trouble," Cole said. "His name is Nacht. I thought he was dead, but if it is him, you're definitely going to be needing the Power of Three."

"Well, then we're going to have to snap Paige out of this somehow," Phoebe said.

"Leo, please orb to the Elders, and see if you can find out what we can do to get Paige back," Piper said.

"And get some details on Nacht. I'll tell you guys what I know, but it's not much," Cole said.

Leo orbed out without another word. This whole thing was too disturbing. In all his years as a Whitelighter he'd never felt a nothing like what he'd felt when he'd touched Paige. This time he was going to get some answers from the Elders. The future of his family depended on it.

"This is insane," Phoebe said to the empty attic as she flipped through the thick pages of the Book of Shadows. Her frustration was growing with every passing moment of complete darkness, the extended night working its way into her veins. Phoebe had been through the book three times but had found no mention of Silas or Nacht. The Book of Shadows had never failed her before, and she hoped it wasn't about to start now.

"So let me get this straight, Nacht has tried this before?" Piper said, walking into the room with Cole. She carried two cups of steaming coffee and handed one to Phoebe. Phoebe inhaled the calming scent and sighed. Nothing like aromatherapy to calm the nerves, even if it was just slightly.

"Eons ago," Cole said, nodding. He pushed his hands into his pants pockets and scowled. "Legend had it that a coven of powerful witches vanquished him, but I guess that was just a rumor."

"The supernatural grapevine is so unreliable," Piper said facetiously. She took a sip of her coffee and looked at Phoebe. "Find anything?"

"Nothing, nada, zip, zilch," Phoebe said, feeling helpless. "I don't understand it. There's always *something*."

"There's always sunrise too," Piper replied.

"Silas probably isn't in there because he always kept a low

profile—until now," Cole said. "He never had the power to come up against a Halliwell, and he wasn't stupid enough to try."

"Well, it seems he's finally *got* the power," Piper said, "and a nifty new friend."

"Ugh! I can't take this anymore!" Phoebe said, slamming the book closed.

"Come on, sweetie, take a break," Piper said, rubbing Phoebe's back with her free hand. "We won't get anywhere if we're all on edge."

Piper and Phoebe settled onto the love seat to sip their coffee while Cole sat down in the chair across from them. Phoebe pulled her legs up under her and waited for the caffeine to kick in. She could definitely use a little jolt right now; she just wished it were going to be a jolt of hope instead of energy. With Paige sleeping like the dead downstairs, Leo being gone for almost an hour, and the distressing sounds of the city growing ever closer, the manor was feeling fairly hope-free. Even Cole's presence was somehow less reassuring than usual.

"Did you try to wake Paige up again?" Phoebe asked him. The first time they'd attempted it, Paige had moaned and groaned until they couldn't take it anymore.

"She was snoring, so we thought we'd let her be and come up here for a while," Piper replied, wrapping her arms around her knees. She shook out her hair so that it fanned over her shoulders and tucked her chin, making her look like a vulnerable little girl. "If Leo comes back with good news, maybe we can try again."

"Hey, she'll be all right," Phoebe said, figuring if she said it aloud, she might start to believe it herself. She reached out and smoothed her sister's hair back so she could see her face. "We've been through tougher times than this before."

"How many times do you think we've said that over the past five or so years?" Piper asked flatly.

"Too many," Phoebe replied.

A swirl of light appeared before them, and then Leo was there, his face lined with concern. Phoebe, Piper, and Cole looked up at him without moving.

"Anyone else just get a feeling of insta-dread?" Phoebe asked, putting her coffee cup aside.

"We couldn't find Silas or Nacht in the Book of Shadows," Piper told Leo, lowering her legs. "From the look on your face I'm guessing you have an explanation."

"Yeah, and it's not a good one," Leo replied, causing Phoebe's heart to thump with foreboding for the hundredth time that morning. If it could even be called a morning with no sun. She had given herself a headache wondering about that one.

"When I told them Cole's theory about Nacht, they were even more disturbed. This demon hasn't stepped foot . . . or hoof, actually, out of the underground in five hundred years."

"He must have been hiding in one of the more remote realms," Cole said. "We all thought he was dead."

"That's why he's not in the book," Phoebe said. "His last appearance on earth predates even Melinda Warren."

"Wait a second, hooves? This thing has hooves?" Piper asked, her forehead wrinkling.

"So why the long hiatus from evildoing?" Phoebe asked, choosing not to think about the hooves herself.

"Because Nacht is not an evildoer by nature. He himself has no taste for killing. All he cares about is bringing forth eternal night," Leo replied. "Apparently this can only be accomplished on the winter solstice once every—"

"Five hundred years." Piper finished his sentence, standing up. "Gotta love the way round numbers always seem to factor in."

"Okay, but if he doesn't have his own bloodlust, then why bring on the dark?" Phoebe asked.

"Power," Cole said, looking Phoebe in the eye. "He does have a lust for power."

"Exactly," Leo said.

"So what does Paige's condition have to do with any of this?" Piper asked.

"That must be where Silas comes in," Cole said. "His powers must have grown over the past century. If he's developed it to the point where he can take away people's wills, they'll just be able to serve up humanity on a silver platter."

"That's exactly what the Elders think he's doing. I told them about what I felt when I tried to heal Paige, and they believe he's taking people's essences, basically erasing their wills," Leo told them. "If Nacht and Silas can give the demon world eternal darkness plus a human race that won't even fight back—"

"The demons will be free to kill, maim, turn us into a slave race . . . ," Cole said.

"All the factions of the demon underworld will bow down to them," Leo said. "They're going to make this world theirs. . . ."

"And then Nacht is going to crown himself king," Cole said.

Phoebe's stomach suddenly rejected the coffee she'd been salivating for since she'd woken up.

"Okay, so Silas sucked out Paige's essence," Piper said, clearly trying to get a handle on one piece of bad news at a time.

"And without it, there's no Power of Three," Leo said, pressing his fists together.

"Well, if Nacht is as powerful as Cole says, we're gonna need it," Piper said, walking toward the book. "Let's see if we can find anything in here about restoring essences."

Piper started to flip from the back of the book forward and was only about twenty pages in when she flattened it open in front of her. Phoebe felt her heart give a leap of hope.

"Here's something," Piper said. "'To restore one's essence,'" she read. "'Unfortunately there is no potion or spell to restore the essence once it has been liberated.'"

"Okay, *that's* helpful," Phoebe said tartly.

"'The only way one's essence can be restored is for the person to be shocked back into caring about something—a cause, a person, a fight.'" Piper read on, gripping the sides of the podium that the book lay upon. " 'This should not be difficult to accomplish if the person felt strongly about something before the essence was taken. But the longer the person is separated from his or her essence, the more difficult restoration becomes.'"

Piper and Phoebe looked at Leo, who lifted his shoulders. "Well, it sounds good to me. Paige cares about a lot of things: the Charmed Ones, her sisters, innocents—"

"Yes! Right!" Phoebe said, clasping her hands together. "But she didn't come out of it when she saw us, so what does that mean?"

"Well . . . the book says she needs to be *shocked* out of it," Cole said slowly, walking toward them. "So maybe if one of you were in danger—"

At that moment a heart-stopping scream pierced Phoebe's chest. It was so loud it could have been right in the attic with her. She ran to the window and shoved it open. On the street below, right in front of the manor, a young woman cowered against a parked car. Standing right across the road from her was a tall demon, cloaked in green robes, brandishing a blue energy ball.

"Piper!" Phoebe called.

Piper ran over to the window and froze the street, just as the demon released the energy ball. Time stopped: the woman shielding her face, the demon with its lips curled back over a toothless mouth, the energy ball hovering in the sky.

"It's a slivash. They kill for sport," Cole said, leaning over Phoebe's shoulder.

"Why didn't you blow him up?" Phoebe demanded, eyes wide as she looked at Piper.

"We have to shock Paige? Well, here's our chance."

Piper grabbed Phoebe's hand and raced out of the room, down two flights of stairs, and into the parlor. She grabbed Paige's shoulders and shook her as hard as she could until Paige finally opened her eyes.

"Come on, sweetie, we're going outside," Piper said, hauling Paige up.

"Um, Piper, I don't know if this is such a good idea," Phoebe said, hopping out of the way so Piper wouldn't step on her foot as she staggered under Paige's weight.

"She's right, Piper," Leo said. "Using an innocent this way—"

"You said it yourself that Paige cares about innocents. It's not like I'm going to let the girl *die*. We're just going to save her in front of Paige, that's all," Piper said, trying to steady Paige so she'd stand on her own. Unfortunately, she kept falling over, leaning her small frame against Piper's side. "Now why don't you do something useful and orb us outside before that demon unfreezes?"

Phoebe shrugged at Leo, and he grabbed them both, orbing all three sisters to the street. When she found her feet on solid ground, Phoebe looked from the demon to the girl and turned to Piper. Cole soon joined them, having walked out the front door the old-fashioned way.

"What's the plan here exactly?" Phoebe asked.

"Okay, Leo, Cole, you hold Paige up," Piper said, transferring her youngest sister's limp form from her own shoulder to her husband's. Cole and Leo strung Paige's arms over their shoulders and held her up between them. "Phoebe, you do your thing on Mr. Demon Man, and I'll pull the girl outta the way. Got it?"

"It's a plan. Not a good plan, but a plan," Phoebe said,

trudging over and placing herself right in front of the demon.

"Ready?" Piper called out.

Phoebe nodded, and Piper raised her hands, unfreezing the scene. She pulled the screaming girl to the ground, and the energy ball smashed into the car, sending shards of windshield glass exploding over the street. The demon saw Phoebe standing in front of him and pulled back, surprised.

"Hiya," Phoebe said with a smile. Then she levitated and landed a kick right up through the demon's jaw. He reeled back, letting out a primal growl, but quickly recovered. Phoebe was taken off guard and never saw the backhand coming. The demon leveled her into the asphalt, and every one of Phoebe's bones shook at impact.

"Piper!" she called out, rolling over slowly.

Piper sat up just as another energy ball sailed toward her. The girl at her side jumped up, right into the projectile's path, and before Piper could freeze anything, the energy ball grazed the girl's arm. The girl cried out in pain and then fainted to the ground. Meanwhile the demon advanced on Phoebe, who was still trying to catch her breath. Both Piper and Phoebe looked to Paige for help, but Paige was just standing there, her blank stare only growing blanker.

"It's not working!" Phoebe called out.

"Piper, do something," Cole cried, watching the demon advance on the love of his life.

"Oh, forget it!" Piper said, frustrated. With a wave of her hands, she blew the demon to bits.

"Think you could have waited a little longer?" Phoebe asked sarcastically, pushing herself into a seated position.

"Leo," Piper said, waving him over as she checked the girl's wound. Even from where Phoebe was sitting it looked pretty nasty.

Cole took all of Paige's weight, lowered her gently to the ground, and leaned her up against a lightpost while Leo joined Piper. He crouched over the girl and quickly healed her arm. She woke up again and looked up at Piper and Leo fearfully.

"It's all right, he's gone," Piper said. She helped the girl up and dusted off her sleeve. "You should probably head home."

"Uh . . . thanks," the girl said, holding her head. Phoebe's heart went out to her. That whole experience had to be fairly freaksome for a person who had probably never seen a demon before. As the girl started off down the street, she staggered slightly and had to reach out for a parking meter to steady herself.

"Leo, maybe you should make sure she gets there," Phoebe said, finally able to stand.

"Are you okay?" Leo asked her.

Phoebe nodded, letting out a little cough that hurt throughout her body. She tried not to wince so that Leo would just go already. Phoebe was afraid their innocent would faint again, and then she'd be demon easy pickin's.

Leo took off at a jog after the girl. Phoebe dragged her sore body over to Paige and Cole, meeting Piper at their side. The eerie smile had returned to Paige's lips as she stared across the street.

Phoebe's heart felt as if it were slowly cracking down the center. "I'm really scared," she said.

"Me too," Piper replied, reaching over and smoothing Paige's hair behind her ear. "If that didn't knock Paige out of this—"

Both sisters watched Paige's placid face, neither one of them wanting to finish the sentence, but the words hung in the air around them, like a thickening fog.

If that didn't knock Paige out of this . . . nothing will.

• • •

Confused and exhausted, wondering what everyone seemed so upset about, Paige slumped back into the couch. Phoebe sat at the table working on a spell, her forehead wrinkled in concentration, while Piper and Leo flitted around her like a couple of crazed birds, chattering with each other, pacing around the parlor. It all looked meaningless and tiresome to Paige. She watched through a hazy mist, her mind working slowly, not even trying to catch up to Piper's rambling or Leo's repeated concerns.

"Maybe we should turn on the TV again," Piper said, looking down at Paige. "Maybe she'll see something that will wake her up."

I'm awake, Paige thought absently. *You guys shook me like a carton of orange juice to make sure of that . . . remember?*

Somewhere in the back of her mind, Paige realized she'd just made a funny. A few minutes later the joke made it to the front of her mind, and her mouth let out a chuckle.

Piper and Leo both looked down at her as if she'd just thrown up, they looked that surprised.

"Something funny, Paige?" Piper asked, sounding almost hopeful.

Paige took a deep breath and lifted her shoulders. She already couldn't remember what had made her laugh. She looked up at her sister until looking up started to take too much effort, and her gaze dropped to roughly the height of Piper's waist.

"How's the spell coming, Phoebe?" Piper asked.

"Okay, I think," Phoebe said, biting her lip. "But it's not going to do us much good if it's just you and me."

"Well, we'll deal with that when the time comes," Piper said. She walked over to the TV and flipped it on. Paige heard hovering helicopters and sirens, heard some woman shouting into a microphone. When she didn't turn to face the TV, Leo came over, picked up her ankles, and turned her until she was resting back against the arm of the couch, the TV in front of her.

"Look!" Piper said, throwing out a hand toward the TV. "People are out there setting fires . . . beating each other . . . getting themselves killed, Paige. Does none of this bother you?"

Paige blinked, watching the action on the screen. A few dozen men pushed and pulled at a light-covered Christmas tree in the center of a traffic square until it finally fell over onto a parked car. Lightbulbs popped, the crash was huge, and the car's alarm blared through the TV's speakers. The men cheered, jumping up and down around the felled tree in a bizarre victory dance.

"What is wrong with people?" Piper said, turning away from the TV.

"Fear does strange things to them," Leo replied. "Look, Paige! Doesn't this touch you at all?"

Paige blinked at the screen. Leo seemed to think that she should be feeling something, but she didn't. She felt nothing at the sight of a child crying, nothing when she saw a group of men attack a defenseless older man. Nothing.

She just didn't care.

Piper threw up her hands and let them drop down at her sides. "I give up."

"It's like there's nothing in there," Cole said. He leaned down in front of Paige and waved his hands in front of her face.

Paige stared at him blankly. *He's so weird,* she thought.

Now he poked her arm—lightly at first, then harder and harder. Paige registered the fact that it hurt, but she didn't have the will to reach up and stop him. She merely sighed and slumped farther down in the couch. Cole laughed and looked at Phoebe like a little kid who'd just found his first washed-up jellyfish: *fascinating.*

"Cole, stop it," Phoebe said, looking up from her spell. "She's our sister, not a toy."

Cole's face fell. "Just trying to figure out how to get her back."

"Well, while poking her is a new idea, it doesn't seem to be working," Piper said. "Any other suggestions?"

Before anyone could answer, Nacht and Silas shimmered into the room, appearing between Paige and the rest of her family. Piper and Leo jumped, and Phoebe let out a little shout of surprise, but Paige didn't turn her head from the TV.

"I have one," Silas said. "You can die."

Paige watched absently as Nacht reached up and whacked Leo clear across the room, where he fell unconscious. Cole rushed him, but the demon tossed him through the nearest window like a Frisbee, shattering the glass. Piper went to raise her hands to blow them into oblivion, but Nacht raised his own hand, projecting a bluish purple shield that deflected Piper's power. It shot off the shield and destroyed the plant behind Piper, showering everyone in the room with dirt and leaves. While Piper was still stunned, Silas grabbed her from behind, securing her hands.

Phoebe launched an assault at Nacht, levitating into the air and trying a roundhouse kick, but the powerful demon reached up, grabbed her leg, and pulled her down. Paige watched it all happen with uninterested detachment.

"Paige!" Phoebe called out as Nacht drew her to him. "Paige! Help us!"

Paige was numb to Phoebe's desperation. There was no fear stirred in her heart, no reaction in her mind that this was not good. All she did was sit back, detached, and watch as Nacht squeezed Phoebe in his arms until the breath left her and her head lolled forward.

Huh. Wonder if she's dead, Paige thought absently. There was no part of her that cared.

"I don't know how you got out of the club, but I thank you for making us find you," Silas said as Piper struggled against him. "Now I'll have the essences of two more Charmed Ones. That should make me indestructible."

"Paige!" Piper shouted. "Wake the heck up!"

I am awake, Paige thought. *Why does everybody keep saying that to me?*

With that, Silas shimmered out. Nacht laughed a horrible, throaty laugh, hovering over Paige.

"Thank you, Charmed One," he said. "You've been most helpful."

He shimmered from the room as well, taking a lifeless Phoebe with him and leaving a lifeless Paige, Cole, and Leo behind.

Piper struggled against the binds that held her wrists together behind her back, but it was no use. This wasn't your average rope or even your average set of handcuffs. Silas had worked some kind of mystical demon mojo on the thick silver bracelets that were attached to the wall by a long chain. They felt as if they were made of iron. Her arms would not budge, and that meant she couldn't use her powers.

Tired from the exertion, Piper leaned back against the cool, jagged wall of the cave Silas had shimmered her into. She was seated on a thick rock, her legs bound as well, and the cold surface seemed to seep right through the back of her jeans. It was freezing in the small dark room. The pitch-black sky was visible through an opening off to Piper's right. Somewhere nearby water dripped at a steady pace, and two fiery torches cast shadows that played along the walls. Two demons with glowing red eyes and slime-covered black skins stood in the far corners, their black hoods pulled up to cover their faces. Piper had no idea where she was, she had no idea if Leo or Phoebe or Paige was still alive, and she'd never felt so alone.

"Don't worry, your sister will be here shortly," Silas said as if reading her mind. "It will be much more satisfying if I take you both at once." He stood across the cave from her in a black-as-night suit, his hands clasped behind his back. Piper narrowed her eyes at him but said nothing.

Suddenly Nacht shimmered into the room with Phoebe hanging limply in his arms. Piper's heart caught in her throat at the sight of her helpless sister, and she strained forward, to no avail.

"She is alive," Nacht said, his voice rumbling against the walls. "For now."

He and Silas quickly bound Phoebe to the wall next to Piper and leaned her back against the rock. Silas held his hands over the cuffs and closed his eyes, muttering the same incantation he'd used on Piper's binds. His palms glowed momentarily, and then he lifted his hands away, satisfied.

"It looks as if the reign of the Charmed Ones is officially over. I thought that just having one of you would be enough, but the power I received from your sister was like nothing I've ever felt before. I assume you two will yield the same. What can I say? I get greedy." As he spoke, Silas stepped to the center of the dirt-covered cave floor next to Nacht. "Don't worry. Once I steal your essences our friends will kill you," he said, gesturing at the demons in the corners. "Our darkness has already spread through California and the Northwest, and it will only grow more with each triumph of evil. Soon the entire world will be plunged into eternal night. I'm sure witches with souls as pure as yours won't want to be alive to see what's coming next."

"You're forgetting one thing," Piper said, hoping her voice sounded more confident than she actually felt. "There are three of us. You've only got two."

Silas scoffed, and Nacht let out a belly laugh that shook the torches in their slips. Piper's heart pounded as she stared them down defiantly.

"Paige is a powerful witch," she said, lifting her chin. "You're underestimating her."

"I believe it is you who are mistaken," Silas said, taking a few steps toward Piper. "Your sister is not as powerful as you believe."

"She'll come to rescue us," Piper said, staring him in the eye. "And the second I'm out of these cuffs we're gonna vanquish your sorry ass."

"Piper?" Phoebe muttered weakly, lifting her head.

Piper's heart soared with irrational hope when she saw her sister stirring. Two Charmed Ones was always better than one.

"It's okay, honey, I'm here," Piper said as Phoebe awoke.

"Oh, good, you're up," Silas said with a smile, turning to Phoebe. "I can't take your essence without your full attention."

"Where are we?" Phoebe asked, still confused.

"Don't worry, sweetie. Everything's going to be fine," Piper told her.

Silas's smile grew so slowly it was almost maddening. "I don't think so," he said. Piper watched as Phoebe came to fully and took in their surroundings. "You see, it was all too easy to take your sister's essence," he told them. "Normally a being with such power and purpose as a Charmed One is purported to have would put up much more of a struggle. Your Paige was ripe for the plucking. I caught her at her most vulnerable, at a moment when all she wanted to do was lose herself. I just helped her along."

A shiver of foreboding skittered over Piper's skin, and she looked at Phoebe.

"That doesn't sound good," Piper said quietly.

Silas stood before them, bowed his head, and began to chant.

Piper struggled against her binds again, hoping for a miracle.

"Paige is going to snap out of it," Phoebe said, an edge in her voice as she watched Silas. "She's going to come for us."

But even as Phoebe said it, Piper knew she didn't believe it. She knew because she herself was starting not to believe it.

Leo lifted his head and winced against the pain that told him just to lie down and go back to sleep. The moment he saw the wreckage in the parlor, however, he jumped up, the throbbing in his skull the last thing on his mind. A chair had been knocked over, a window shattered, dirt and leaves and branches covered the surface of the floor and the table, and the wicker pot that once held the tree in the corner was still smoking. Piper, Phoebe, and Cole were nowhere to be seen . . . and Paige was still lounging on the couch.

"Paige!" Leo said, falling to his knees in front of her, his pulse racing wildly. He grabbed both her arms and hoisted her up so that she was sitting straight. "Paige! What happened to the others?"

Paige lifted her shoulders slowly. "Cole went out the window. Nacht and Silas took Piper and Phoebe," she said. "They shimmered."

Leo was a pacifist by nature, but he felt as if he were going to erupt right there. He stood up, releasing his grip on Paige's arms, and rushed outside to find Cole. The moment he saw his friend, his breath caught in his throat. There was a lot of blood. Leo dropped to his knees and healed Cole's wounds. It took longer than usual—his condition was serious—but Cole finally came to. He took one look at Leo and sat up straight.

"Phoebe?" he asked.

"They're gone. She and Piper," Leo said.

Together they went back to the parlor and confronted the

languishing Paige. Leo took a deep breath, hoping his initial explosion of frustration would burn off. But calm didn't come so easily. No matter what Silas had done to Paige, no matter what he had taken from her, he couldn't believe that she had let this happen.

He crouched in front of her again and hoisted her to her feet. "These are your sisters, Paige," he said, holding her at arm's length and glaring into her eyes. "How could you just sit there and let them be taken?"

Paige simply stared back at him blankly. *She's not in there,* Leo remembered with a shudder. *This is totally pointless.*

"She can't help us, Leo," Cole said. "We're on our own."

Leo stood up again and told himself to calm down. Cole was right. They themselves had to help Piper and Phoebe. The fate of the world depended on it, not to mention the fate of his own heart.

"Can you sense them?" Cole asked.

Leo closed his eyes and breathed in and out deliberately, reaching out with his heart into the ether to try to sense Piper and Phoebe. All he could do was hope that Nacht hadn't taken them to the underworld or he would never be able to find them.

Suddenly his heart squeezed, and his eyes flew open. "Piper," he whispered, relieved even as he felt her fear.

"Let's go," Cole said.

Leo grabbed Cole's arm, wrapped his other arm around Paige, and orbed out. When Leo's feet hit solid ground again, he found himself in a dark, dank, freezing cold cave. He saw Piper and Phoebe chained against a wall surrounded by demons and quickly yanked Paige and Cole behind a protrusion in the rock to hide. Together he and Cole leaned Paige into a ledge and peeked around the corner to assess the situation.

A pair of hooded demons were advancing on Piper and Phoebe with daggers drawn. All Leo could see of them was the black, slimy skin of their hands and their long white claws. Silas stood between the two demons chanting, while Nacht hovered in the corner, seemingly a spectator to the proceedings.

Leo's breath caught in his throat as the demons held the daggers to Piper's and Phoebe's throats. They both held their heads back and stared at Silas bravely, defiantly, but Leo could sense their terror. As Leo watched helplessly, Silas raised his hands, palms up, the chant growing louder.

"We have to help them," Cole whispered, starting forward.

Leo grabbed his arm to stop him. "You go in there and you're dead. You're human now, remember?"

"So what? We're just supposed to watch them die?" Cole whispered.

"No," Leo said, "I have a better idea."

He grabbed Paige and made her face the ritual in the cave, grasping her shoulders to hold her up.

"Look, Paige!" Leo shouted. "Look at what's happening! These are your sisters! They love you, and you love them! You can't let this happen!"

Leo's strategy worked. The demons with the daggers turned away from Piper and Phoebe and, snarling menacingly, advanced on him, Cole, and Paige. Silas, however, continued to chant, and Leo saw a swirling orb of color appear between his palms.

"The ritual," Cole said. "He's going to take their essences."

"Paige!" Phoebe called out. "Paige! Help us!"

Leo looked at the demons creeping toward him, saw Nacht sweeping his way, looked into Paige's lifeless eyes, and realized it was over. He'd failed his wife, failed Cole, failed the Charmed Ones, failed in his duty. They all were about to die.

• • •

"Paige!" Piper and Phoebe screamed in unison. "Paige! Please! Wake up!"

Oh, man, they're screaming again, Paige thought, wishing Leo would just sit her down again and let her be.

"Look, Paige," Cole said. He reached over, grabbed the sides of her face, and turned her so that she was looking directly into Phoebe's eyes from across the room. "Look at them! Help them!"

Paige stared into Phoebe's desperate eyes and felt a sudden stirring in her chest, a sudden heat more intense than anything she'd felt in the past twenty-four hours.

Okay . . . what's going on? Paige thought.

The warmth spread across her body, down her arms and legs, into her fingers and toes, and as it did, Paige was hit with a million sensations. Fear filled her heart; adrenaline rushed through her veins. All the air rushed out of her, and she gasped as it rushed right back in. She almost crumbled to the ground from the force of it. Suddenly, across the cave, Silas fell to his knees. The orb disappeared from his hands, and he clutched at his heart.

He threw his head back and screamed out in excruciating pain, writhing as if someone were ripping out his insides.

Something slammed into Paige's chest. She was blasted backward as if she'd been hit by a thunderbolt. Her heart was injected with fire, but good fire, warm fire, comforting fire. Her head snapped up; her eyes went wide; her entire body was energized.

"Wow," Paige said out loud, looking at her tingling fingers. Suddenly she felt incredibly, euphorically alive.

The fog was gone. Paige was back. And damn, did it feel good.

"Daggers!" she shouted, thrusting her hands out.

The two daggers the demons were holding appeared in her palms in swirls of light. She reached back and let them fly, hitting both demons directly in their hearts. The demons screamed, clutching at the handles to their own weapons, then disappeared in bursts of black smoke.

Silas struggled to his feet, clearly weakened but determined as ever. The sphere appeared above his hands again as he staggered toward Piper and Phoebe.

"Don't look into the orb!" Paige shouted.

Piper and Phoebe squeezed their eyes shut just as Nacht tossed a fireball in Paige's direction. She orbed out just in time, and the fire exploded against the wall next to Cole's head. Paige reappeared in front of Silas and kicked him square in the stomach. He doubled over, and Paige turned to her sisters.

"Sorry it took me so long."

"No problem, but a little help here?" Piper said, leaning forward to show Paige her cuffs and the chain that held her to the wall.

"Cuffs!" Paige said, holding out her hands.

All the chains and binds that held her sisters were suddenly draped over her arms, and she staggered under the weight. Her knees buckled slightly as Piper and Phoebe stood up.

"Paige, get down!" Phoebe shouted.

Paige hit the ground, and Phoebe levitated, narrowly escaping another flying fireball. While Paige was on the floor, she lost track of Silas, and suddenly he was upon her, dragging her up by the back of her hair. Paige cried out in pain and grasped at one of the chains. As Silas backpedaled with her toward the wall, Paige lifted the chain and whipped it around rodeo style, whacking Silas in the back of the head.

She heard the crack, and Silas suddenly released her. Paige stepped away and looked at Piper.

"A little help here?"

Piper turned and thrust her hands in Silas's direction. He

shouted out at the last second, but it was too late. Silas exploded in a shower of black ash. Paige smiled and slapped her hands together. "Think you can take *my* essence and get away with it?" she asked, looking down at the pile of soot that was Silas. "Ha!"

"Uh . . . you guys?" Phoebe called out.

Paige looked up to find that Phoebe, Leo, and Cole were battling Nacht and getting nowhere fast. The demon, though big and slow, was obviously powerful. He grabbed Cole by the throat and slammed him into the ground, then deflected one of Phoebe's kicks. She went spinning off across the room, and her side crashed into one of the jagged walls. Leo jumped onto Nacht's back, wrapping his arms around the thing's neck, but Nacht simply staggered back, crunching Leo against the wall. Leo fell limply to the ground, the wind knocked out of him.

"All right, Nacht, I appreciate what you're trying to do with this eternal night thing, but I'm a day person," Piper said. "Sorry."

She reached up and threw her hands at Nacht . . . and nothing happened. Paige felt her heart thump against her rib cage.

"Uh-oh," Piper said.

Phoebe pushed herself up from the floor, and she and Paige both walked up next to Piper as Nacht let out a huge, booming laugh. His head tipped back, and he bared his fangs to the ceiling, reveling in his mirth.

"What's so funny, Barney?" Paige said, eyeing his purple skin.

"You think you can defeat me with a measly power like that?" he said. "That is all the powerful Charmed Ones have brought to fight a mighty demon like Nacht?"

"No, not quite," Phoebe said, pulling a slip of paper out of her back pocket.

That's right! Phoebe wrote a spell! Paige thought triumphantly. Nacht was about to eat his words. She and Piper gathered around Phoebe, and together the Charmed Ones began to read.

We call on the powers of goodness and light,
Take this demon from our sight.
End this mystical evil night,
Bring back the day, set time to right.

Paige looked up at Nacht, but nothing happened. He simply stood before them, a look on his bulbous face that passed for a demon smirk.

"It's not working," Piper said.

"Are you done yet?" Nacht said, advancing on them.

"Come on, you guys, keep going!" Paige shouted, thrusting out her hand. Phoebe reached both hands out and clutched her sisters'. Paige felt the power of their connection surge through her. She never felt as close to her sisters as she did when they were connected like this. Suddenly, with Phoebe's hand in hers and her sisters' power coursing through her veins, she knew she was where she was supposed to be. She felt invincible, a far cry from the numbness she'd been experiencing all day.

We call on the powers of goodness and light,
Take this demon from our sight.

A swirl of wind kicked up around Paige, Piper, and Phoebe, whipping their hair across their faces, throwing dirt up from the floor to pelt their skin. Nacht suddenly froze in place. Paige struggled to keep her eyes open in the commotion. She squinted through the wind and light and silt to watch Nacht as she continued to chant.

End this mystical evil night,
Bring back the day, set time to right.

Suddenly Nacht's head snapped back, but this time he was not laughing. His arms flew into the air, and he started to shake. A deafening, guttural growl escaped his lips, shaking the very foundations of the cave.

It's working, Paige thought. *It's working!*

We call on the powers of goodness and light,
Take this demon from our sight.
End this mystical evil night,
Bring back the day, set time to right.

Nacht trembled more and more violently until he finally fell to his knees, his arms still raised. Finally, with one last defiant cry, his entire body crumbled to the ground in front of the Charmed Ones. A blast of white-blue light threw the sisters back into the cave wall, and as they hit the ground, Nacht vanished into the ether.

Instantly light poured through the yawning opening of the cave, blinding Paige as she fought for breath. She instinctively held her hand up to shield her eyes from the light, but then realization hit her: She and her sisters had won. They had brought back the sun, saved the world. She wasn't going to hide from it.

"Leo?" Phoebe called out, rushing to Cole's side.

Leo quickly healed Cole, and as Cole awoke, he glanced around, confused. "Thanks . . . again," he said to Leo as Phoebe helped him up.

"Everyone okay?" Leo asked.

"Fine," Piper said, standing and dusting off her clothes.

Paige pushed herself up with both hands and looked at her sisters. Suddenly both descended on her to grab her up in a big bear hug.

"You're back!" Phoebe said, burying her face in Paige's hair.

"Yep," Paige said. She hugged them to her, reveling in their warmth, their closeness.

"You had us worried for a while there," Piper said.

"It was so weird. It was like I was there, but I didn't *feel anything* so I had no motivation to *do* anything," Paige told them with a shudder. "I can't believe I just let Silas and Nacht take you. I'm really sorry, you guys."

"Hey, there's nothing to be sorry for," Piper said, pulling back. She ran her hand over Paige's hair and tucked it behind her ear tenderly. "That jerk put a spell on you. It wasn't your fault."

"Still, I think a part of me . . . a small part . . . wanted to disappear—at least for a little while," Paige said, her stomach turning as she bit her lip. "I think he may have sensed that in me."

Phoebe and Piper exchanged a look but smiled. "The important thing is you came through when we needed you," Phoebe told her. "You came back."

Paige smiled, feeling as light as air. For the first time in a long time she felt relaxed, loose, and happy. She'd been bogged down for so long, feeling tense and unappreciated, she'd forgotten how *good* it could feel to be needed.

"Where would you guys be without me?" Paige asked, looping her arms around her sisters' necks.

Leo and Cole followed them as they walked toward the light at the edge of the cave. They stood in the opening, looking down at the easy slope that led to the trees below. In the distance Paige could see the Golden Gate Bridge and knew that they weren't far from home. Paige tipped her face toward the sun, the light washing over her and infusing her with happiness.

"Ready to head back to the manor?" Leo asked.

Piper and Phoebe looked at Paige, smiling, and Paige shrugged. "I do have a lot of chores to do," she said. "But I am not doing windows anymore. That is just too much to ask."

Phoebe and Piper laughed and hugged Paige. She wrapped her arms around them and enveloped them in her swirling white light to orb them home. At that moment she realized she had never felt so loved or so strong.

Her future was bright. She was a sister, a friend, a Charmed One, and she wouldn't have it any other way.

"Merry Christmas, everyone!" Paige called out, plopping down under the new tree in her white flannel pajamas. She had a bright red Santa cap on her head and green and red striped socks on her feet. No one was going to be able to accuse Paige Matthews of missing the spirit of the season.

"Merry Christmas, Paige," Leo said, walking into the room with a trayful of coffee and muffins. Piper reached up from the chair where she was lounging and took a steaming cup in both hands.

Phoebe yawned and adjusted her languishing position on the couch, bringing both feet up onto the cushions. "Okay, somebody give me a present!" she demanded with a fake petulant frown.

Paige, Piper, and Leo all smiled slyly, exchanging a mischievous look. "This year you get only one," Piper said, sipping at her coffee. "We all chipped in."

Phoebe sat up straight, showing her first energy spurt of the morning. "One present?" she asked, her brown eyes wide. "But I've been a very good girl!"

Paige laughed and pushed herself up from the floor. She

grabbed Phoebe's present from behind the tree and hauled it over to her. Phoebe's eyes widened even further when she saw the size of the box her one present was coming in.

"Okay, maybe you're forgiven," she said, reaching her arms up and around the box as Paige placed it in her lap.

Everyone watched as Phoebe yanked off the silver bow and tore at the wrapping paper. She managed to expose enough of the box to read the label and see a large portion of the photo depicting her new laptop computer.

"Omigod, you guys!" Phoebe screeched. "This is awesome! Thank you so much!" Piper, Paige, and Leo laughed as Phoebe ripped the rest of the paper to shreds and read the computer's features from the side of the box. "This is like ten times faster than my old one!" she said, bouncing in her seat just like a little kid who'd just opened her first Barbie Dream House. "Thank you, thank you, thank you!"

She leaned over to give Paige a peck on the cheek, and Paige gave Phoebe a quick squeeze, giddiness overcoming her. There was nothing she liked better than giving gifts and seeing her family's reactions. After everything that had happened in the last few days, Christmas was a much-needed release. The Halliwell/Matthews clan was reveling in the pure joy the day brought, no one more than Paige, who was happy to be feeling anything at all.

"Piper next," Paige said, grabbing a smaller gift from under the tree. She passed it over to Piper, who put her coffee aside.

"Thank you, Paige," she said as she started to open the present. Paige's heart skipped when Piper's face lit up. "A Palm Pilot!" Piper said happily. "I always wanted one of these things."

"Well, since I got your last planner impaled . . . ," Paige said with a shrug.

"Not your fault," Piper said, putting on her serious face momentarily. "But thank you. I love it."

Paige leaned across the table to hug Piper, glad that both her sisters had liked their gifts. Maybe next year she'd be able to buy them presents that weren't replacements for demon-vanquishing casualties.

"Can I go?" Leo asked as Paige sat down again.

"Oh, yeah!" Phoebe said, putting the computer on the floor and pulling her knees up under her chin. She looked at Paige expectantly and grinned. "I can't wait to see this."

Paige's brow furrowed as she looked around at her family. "What?" she asked, sensing the anticipation in the air.

"Well, you're getting only one present too," Piper said with a grin. "It was Leo's idea, so he gets to give it to you."

Leo stood up and pulled something out of the back pocket of his jeans. He smiled at Paige as he reached across the room and handed her a large ivory envelope.

"Okay, not quite as impressive in size as Phoebe's," Paige said, turning the envelope over in her hands.

Phoebe nudged Paige's thigh with her toe, and Paige slid her finger under the envelope flap. She pulled out a large gift certificate from La Spiaga Day Spa and read the message.

"For Paige Matthews, from Piper, Phoebe, and Leo," she read aloud. "One Queen-for-a-Day package. Services include deep tissue massage, manicure and pedicure, facial, sauna, and hours of relaxation at our luxurious facility in the beautiful Sonoma Valley."

Paige's heart warmed at the gesture and the significance behind it. "You guys . . . thank you," she said, holding the gift certificate against her chest.

"You deserve it," Phoebe said sincerely.

"We really do appreciate everything you do, Paige," Piper said.

"All of us," Leo said.

Paige felt her eyes well up with tears and blinked them back. It was Christmas morning, and she wasn't going to turn into a blubbering idiot. She gave Phoebe a big hug, then did the same for Piper and Leo, walking around the coffee table to do so.

"Okay, let's open the rest of the gifts so we can eat!" Paige announced, standing in the middle of the room.

As Phoebe launched herself under the tree to fish out her gift for Piper and Piper went searching for the present she'd bought for Leo, Paige hovered at the edge of the room, laughing and watching the festivities. She looked down at her gift and smiled, running her finger along the gilded emblem for the spa. To her it was as good as real gold.

In that moment Paige knew that she was needed *and* appreciated, loved and cared for. What more could a Charmed One ask for?

Imbolc

by Laura J. Burns

"An entire week off!" Piper Halliwell murmured happily. She pushed her chair back from the desk and sighed in contentment. Life just couldn't get any better than this. She'd been married to the love of her life for almost a year now, and it was everything she'd expected. Leo was warm, and supportive, and always there for her when she needed him.

Well, almost always. Because he was a Whitelighter, he often had to rush off to help innocents—his charges—in trouble. But that was part of what made him so wonderful. Also, Piper knew that if she really needed him, he'd find a way to be with her no matter what.

Plus, she and Leo had been talking about having a baby. She rested one hand on her stomach. She wasn't entirely sure yet, but she thought she might have some good news for him soon. Plan number one for her week off was to buy a home pregnancy test.

She glanced around the cluttered office. Her career was also going well. The club she owned with her sisters, P3, was doing better than ever. In fact they'd finally made enough money to afford the extension Piper had always wanted to build. The club would be closed for seven days, and the contractors had their orders. By this time next week her office would be twice as big, with enough space to put in all the file cabinets and shelves she needed to organize the current chaos. Plus, the ladies' room in the club would be big enough to practically eliminate lines altogether. Piper liked to think of that as her little contribution to women's rights.

She glanced at the framed photo on her desk; her sisters' smiling faces looked back at her. Phoebe and Paige, horsing around during a picnic in Golden Gate Park. In a separate frame she kept a picture of Prue, her older sister. Prue had died not too long ago, fighting the forces of evil. Piper sighed. That was one area of her life that would never feel okay. She would miss Prue forever. And since her sister's death, Piper couldn't help feeling an extra weight on her own shoulders. *She* was the eldest sister now, with all the responsibilities that entailed. Phoebe was more of a free spirit, often consumed with her ex-demon fiancé, Cole, or her various stabs at nine-to-five work. And Paige was still so new to the family and to being a Charmed One. This time last year Piper hadn't even known she had a younger half sister, the result of her mother's love affair with a Whitelighter. Paige was trying her hardest, but she still had a long way to go until she would be the powerful witch she was destined to be. There was so much for her to learn.

At least Prue and Phoebe and I went through all that together, Piper thought to herself, studying Paige's grinning face. *Paige has to come to grips with her powers all by herself.* She wished she could find a way to help her half sister. She encouraged her to practice their craft as much as possible, but she still didn't feel as if she were really helping Paige all that much. Sometimes just being there didn't feel like enough.

Piper stood and took one more look around the office. She

wouldn't be able to get in here once the contractors began work tomorrow.

"I know I'm forgetting something," she muttered to herself. She'd packed up all the important papers—the financial records, the employee files, and anything else she wanted to keep safe from sawdust, paint, and the contractors' general mess. She picked up the photos of her sisters and stuck them into her bag. Then she looked at her datebook.

Leo will kill me if I bring you home, she told the leather-bound book. Her husband wanted her to take a real vacation while the club was closed. He didn't want her even to think about work. But Piper wasn't sure she could bear to leave the planner behind. What if something went wrong? What if a vendor called to check on a delivery date or a famous band called to book a gig? She'd be lost without her datebook. As she reached for it, her gaze fell on the page that held next week's dates, a clean, blank page, with no appointments at all.

"What am I going to do with myself?" Piper said aloud. A vacation *sounded* great, but she knew herself too well. Five days off would drive her crazy. Especially since she'd be spending those days by herself. Phoebe and Paige both would be busy working, and it wasn't as if Whitelighters could take vacations from the witches who needed them. She'd known when she married Leo that they wouldn't be taking too many family trips to exotic locales.

One of the dates on the blank page seemed to draw her gaze. February 2. Piper caught her breath. "Imbolc," she whispered. She rarely remembered the Wiccan sabbats. It was hard enough keeping up with the more traditional holidays, and she and her sisters hadn't been raised in the Wiccan religion. Piper knew only a handful of facts about some of the feast days. Still, she did know that Imbolc was a fertility celebration, the perfect time to start getting ready for motherhood! She didn't want to get her hopes up too soon, but maybe this time next year she would have a witchy little baby!

This is a perfect opportunity, she told herself as she stuffed the datebook into her overflowing bag. *I'll learn how to celebrate Imbolc like a good Wiccan.* Another thought struck her. Maybe this was a fun way for Paige to learn about their craft. *And then I'll teach my sisters how to celebrate it too!*

"Do you know what tomorrow is?" Piper asked in a singsong voice.

Uh-oh, Phoebe thought, *Piper has her kindergarten teacher voice on.* She yawned and took a bite of Mueslix. It was too early to deal with her overachieving sister.

"Well?" Piper asked, an edge creeping into her tone.

"Um . . . Monday?" Phoebe said.

"No," Piper replied. "Well, yes. But that's not what I meant."

From across the kitchen table Paige shot Phoebe a questioning look. "Does she always ask trick questions this early in the morning?" she whispered.

Piper ignored the gibe. "It's February second!" she announced. "You know what that means!"

Phoebe wondered if her sister had lost her mind. "Groundhog Day?" she asked. Paige sneezed.

Piper looked annoyed. "No," she said, rolling her eyes. "Well, yes. But I'm talking about Imbolc. February second is the Wiccan feast of Imbolc. Also known as Oimealg, St. Brigid's Day, and Candlemas."

"Is there going to be a quiz on this?" Paige asked with a teasing grin.

"There just might be, missy." Piper teased her back. "I've decided it's time we all learn about one of the major Wiccan holidays. We are Wiccans after all."

Phoebe groaned. "I knew this was coming," she said.

"What do you mean?" Piper put on an innocent expression, but Phoebe could tell her sister knew exactly what she was talking about.

"I mean that you're not going in to work at P3 all week, so you're looking for some project to fill up your time. And apparently you think it's going to be Imbolc, Paige, and me."

Paige sneezed again.

"Bless you," Piper said distractedly. "I just thought it would be nice to teach Paige about some of the fun traditions that go along with being the Charmed Ones"—she continued—"since she's already seen lots of the dangerous, evil parts of it."

"That's for sure," Paige said. "If I never see another monster, it'll be too soon." She sneezed again.

"What's with the sneezing?" Phoebe asked, concerned.

Paige's brown eyes looked watery. "I think I caught a cold at the office," she said. "But I'm sure it's nothing a little Imbolc celebration won't cure!"

Oh, no, Phoebe thought. *Piper has reeled her in. Now it's going to be all Imbolc for the next two days.* "I can give you a few hours tonight," she said out loud. "But that's all for now. I have an assignment due tomorrow for my psych class."

Piper grinned from ear to ear. "Great!" she exclaimed. "I've been doing some research on the holiday. It'll be so much fun!"

Phoebe couldn't help a smile as she watched her older sister. Piper was usually the down-to-earth, sensible one. It was kind of cool to see her get all excited about this Imbolc thing. Maybe it *would* be fun after all.

"This sucks," Phoebe whined.

Paige felt the same way, but she shot her sister a warning look. Both she and Phoebe had been complaining about the Imbolc preparations ever since they started, and Paige had a feeling that Piper was ready to freeze them both. Or maybe even make them explode.

Phoebe ignored her and kept on complaining. "I have dirt under every single fingernail," she said, glaring at the bowl of acorns on the table in front of her. She was supposed to be gluing them onto branches in order to make magic acorn wands. So far she had one wand finished.

"What's a little dirt?" Piper replied as she dipped candlewicks into a pot of hot wax on the stove. "You're supposed to be thinking about the meaning of Imbolc, not about your manicure."

"Yeah, but I'm more Jon Stewart than Martha Stewart," Phoebe said dryly. "Can't I just sit around and make fun of this stuff? It will take me all night to make wands out of all these stupid acorns."

Paige's head was swimming—the cold had moved into her sinuses, and all she wanted to do was sleep—and the last thing she needed was a fight between her sisters. She took one look at Piper's flashing eyes and decided it was time for some diplomacy.

"Well, I for one can't think about the meaning of Imbolc when I don't even know what it is," she said. "For instance, why am I making these . . . dolls?" Paige regarded the mangled cornhusks on the table in front of her. She'd been twisting them together for what seemed like hours, but none of the husks resembled a doll.

"Brideo'gas," Piper told her.

"What are Brideo'gas?" Phoebe asked.

Piper's cheeks reddened. "They're cornhusk dolls," she replied. "But they're very special dolls."

"Or in my case, very lame dolls," Paige said, turning her head to sneeze. "Do you think it matters if they don't have heads?"

"They're supposed to be symbols of the Maiden," Piper said, "so I think heads would be a good thing."

"What maiden?" Paige asked.

"Witches used to consider Imbolc the feast of Brigid, an Irish fertility goddess," Piper replied. "At this time each year she would prepare for the birth of her son, the sun."

Paige stared blankly at her sister. What did some Irish goddess have to do with anything?

Piper sighed. "It's a metaphor for the seasons," she said, exasperated. "When she gives birth to the sun, spring starts. Even though it takes place in the dead of winter, the holiday is all about preparing for the return of spring."

"It still sounds like Groundhog Day to me," Phoebe muttered.

Paige couldn't help giggling. The whole thing really did seem as pointless as watching some rodent decide whether to sleep late or not. But now Piper was glaring at both of them.

"This is a very important holiday," she said sternly. "It's a mystical celebration of the life that lies dormant through the winter, only to burst forth again in springtime. . ."

As Piper lectured them, Paige caught Phoebe's eye. Behind Piper's back, Phoebe gave an exaggerated yawn. Paige opened her mouth to laugh, but instead she coughed. This cold was really getting the better of her.

". . . the magic of being a woman," Piper was saying. "Women can create life, and Imbolc is a time to celebrate the preparation for a child—Hey!" she snapped, catching Phoebe in a half-jokey eye roll.

Phoebe froze: busted. Paige burst out laughing. Phoebe joined in, embarrassed.

Piper threw up her hands. "I don't know why I even bother," she said. "You two are acting like five-year-olds!"

"Sorry. But with making dolls and magic wands and all, it

kind of seems like a holiday meant for five-year-olds," Phoebe said. "I know you're bored, Piper, but I just can't sit here doing arts and crafts when I have homework to do." Phoebe pushed back her chair and stood up. "I have to go. I promise I'll be back later," she told her sisters, heading for the stairs.

"What about the Imbolc preparations?" Piper cried.

"Piper, I just don't have time tonight," Phoebe told her.

Piper turned pleading eyes to Paige. Paige sneezed. "I'm sorry," she said. "I really have to get to bed. I'll be much more ready to absorb my witchy heritage after some cold medicine and a power nap."

"Great," Piper said. "Now I'm going to have to finish the dolls and the wands by myself. All I wanted was for us to learn about our traditions, how to make dolls and wands and candles—things witches have been doing on Imbolc Eve for hundreds of years."

"Tell you what," Phoebe said to Piper. "When you and Leo have a baby, you can start teaching it to do all this Imbolc stuff. That would be fun!"

Paige caught her breath. The look on Piper's face was clear; the conversation had gone too far. They might not be in the right frame of mind to learn about Imbolc, but Piper *really* wasn't ready to consider a little bundle of Wicca/Whitelighter joy!

Do they know I'm pregnant? Piper wondered, running over Phoebe's words in her mind. She absently dipped the candlewick into the hot wax, over and over. She hadn't been planning to tell anyone until she confirmed her suspicions. But maybe her sisters could tell. . . .

Piper frowned. Her plan for Imbolc fun hadn't gone very well. Paige and Phoebe hadn't paid any attention to her when she tried to get them into the spirit. And if she couldn't even get her sisters to do what she asked, how would she be able to corral a kid? Especially a kid with magical powers? She'd been so focused on wanting to have a baby. She'd never even thought about whether she'd be a good mom. Was she ready?

"Ouch!" Piper cried. She'd dipped the wick a little too energetically and plunged her hand right into the wax. Dropping the half-made candle into the pot, she snatched her hand out and stuck it under the faucet in the sink, using her other hand to turn on the cold water. As the cooling sensation spread over her skin, she frowned. *What kind of mother will I be if I'm this absentminded?* she thought. *I can't even keep myself from getting burned!*

When all the wax was scrubbed from her hands, Piper decided she had enough candles, especially since it seemed she'd be celebrating Imbolc alone tomorrow. She sat at the table and picked up one of Paige's twisted cornhusk Brideo'gas. She took one look at it and snorted. Her sisters might think this crafts stuff was fit only for a first grader, but Piper was willing to bet that most first graders could do a much better job.

She began to construct a head. *I need to calm down,* she thought. *Of course I'm ready to be a mom.* After all, she was able to run a business, have a happy marriage, and save lots of innocents from demons and warlocks and other evil types. How much harder could one little baby be?

Piper tried to imagine her life with a baby: her newly renovated office covered in toys, the piles of baby clothes in the laundry room, a crying infant waking her up in the middle of the night. And warlocks, demons, and all sorts of monsters coming after her, trying to hurt her child. How could any mother protect a baby from the kind of evil that was a part of daily life for a Charmed One?

A feeling of panic rose in her throat. Her hands began to

tingle, but not in the ticklish way they did when she used her powers to freeze things. This was a tingling that rapidly spread up her arms and into her chest, making it hard to breathe.

"Great. Now I'm having a panic attack," she confessed to the doll. Then she realized she was chatting with a cornhusk. "This is crazy," she said, putting the doll on the table.

She pushed back her chair and headed for the cabinet where she kept all her herbs. "Chamomile," she murmured, trying to ignore her pounding heart. "I'll make some tea, I'll get a grip, and I shall stop panicking about motherhood. I don't even know if I'm pregnant yet. I'm freaking out over nothing."

"Did you say something?" A white light filled the kitchen at the same time Piper heard her husband's voice. She jumped in surprise and spun around to see Leo orbing in.

"What?" Piper yelped.

"I thought I heard you talking," Leo said. He took in her fast breathing and her frightened eyes. "Is everything okay?"

"Yes," Piper said quickly. "Of course everything's fine." She took a deep breath and forced herself to smile. She began cleaning up the Imbolc ingredients on the table.

"What's all this?" Leo asked, frowning at the scattered acorns, twigs, and cornhusks.

"Oh, I was trying to get Paige and Phoebe to celebrate Imbolc with me," Piper said. "On Imbolc Eve, we're supposed to make cornhusk dolls called Brideo'gas and then put magic acorn wands in their hands. We make candles and then tomorrow—"

"You burn the dolls and the wands and you see if the ashes reveal any signs of the coming spring." Leo finished her sentence for her.

Piper stared at him, astonished.

"I am a Whitelighter," Leo told her, grinning. "I'm well versed in Wicca."

Piper felt a rush of love for her husband. Her sisters hadn't been too enthusiastic about this holiday, but he might just know more about it than she did. Her panic forgotten, she took Leo's hand and slid onto his lap.

"What other things have you picked up about Imbolc?" she asked.

He wrapped his arm around her waist. "Well, it's a fertility celebration," he said. "It's about the goddess preparing to give birth to the spring. So it's an especially important holiday for pregnant women and women who want to be pregnant." He squeezed her tighter for a moment.

Piper's breath caught in her throat. Did *Leo* know she was pregnant? She didn't want to tell him until she was absolutely positive. She didn't want to get his hopes up if it was a false alarm. She jumped off his lap and concentrated on clearing the table. "Paige and Phoebe aren't very interested in celebrating," she said, making her voice casual. "So I guess I won't bother."

"Okay," Leo replied with a shrug. "But if you want to celebrate Imbolc, I'll be there to help."

"Maybe next year," Piper said.

"Whatever you want, honey."

Piper smiled as she wiped down the counter. Even if she wasn't entirely ready to be a mom, it was okay. Because she had a wonderful, dependable husband to help her. Leo would be the best father in history.

"You know what other holiday comes in February?" Leo asked.

Piper shot him a smile. "Um . . . Presidents Day."

Leo chuckled. "I was thinking of something a little more romantic. Valentine's Day."

"Best day of the year," Piper said.

"And this year I have a surprise for you," Leo told her. "Since it's our first Valentine's as husband and wife, I thought we could celebrate by going away for the weekend." He handed Piper a brochure.

She glanced at it, taking in the photo of a charming vine-covered cottage by a lake.

"It's a bed-and-breakfast in Monterey. I talked to the Elders, and they said they would watch over my charges for two days," Leo told her.

"All your charges?" Piper asked. She threw her arms around her husband.

"All but one. One very special witch," Leo said. "I want to make sure I'm the only one watching over her." He buried his face in her hair.

Piper smiled. That would be the perfect time to tell Leo that they were going to be parents. She looked up into his beautiful blue eyes. "I can't wait," she said.

"Happy Imbolc," Paige said to Piper the next morning. She felt bad for bailing on her sister in the middle of all the preparations. In fact she felt bad in general. Her head was pounding, she had to blow her nose every two minutes, and she'd developed a cough.

Piper glanced up from the paper she was reading. "Yeah, you too." She didn't even crack a smile.

Yikes, Paige thought, *Piper is even madder at me than I thought she'd be.* She collapsed into a seat at the kitchen table and put her head down on her arms. "Sorry we were so grumpy last night," she said with a sniffle.

Piper sighed. "It's okay. I know you're sick."

"Seriously," Paige said, "I think my head is going to explode. I guess I should call in sick to work." She didn't like missing work at Social Services, where she was a social worker. And it seemed to be happening more and more now that she had to run off at a moment's notice to fulfill her Charmed duties. But she didn't want to pass this cold on to her coworkers. "I took some cold medicine I found in the bathroom upstairs."

"Good," Piper replied absently.

Paige studied her sister. Piper was really out of it. *Maybe she had a fight with Leo,* Paige thought. *This has to be more than Phoebe and me dissing her Imbolc plans.*

"Well, I'm going to go back to bed," Paige said. She pushed back her chair and orbed. When the white light faded, Paige found herself sitting on a bed in a strange room.

"Whoa," she said. "What just happened?"

She looked around, taking in the small room. Clothes were strewn about on the wooden floor. An empty pizza box sat on a low table in the corner. Nothing looked as if it had been cleaned for at least a year. Or smelled like it either. "Ewww." Paige wrinkled her nose. "If it stinks to me with this cold, I can't imagine how bad it really smells."

Still, there was something about the room that looked familiar. Paige got up and crossed to the window. She pulled aside the flannel sheet that was tacked up as a curtain and peered outside.

"No way!" she cried. The view was unmistakable: an alleyway with two other buildings crowding together five feet away. And just visible between the buildings was the top of the Transamerica Building. "It's my old apartment!"

Paige dropped the "curtain" and spun around. It might be her old apartment, but clearly someone else lived here now. And to judge by the sound of the shower running in the tiny bathroom off the bedroom, that someone was at home. "I have to get out of here," Paige murmured.

She willed herself to orb back to the kitchen at Halliwell Manor. Nothing happened.

Surprised, Paige closed her eyes and concentrated harder. Still nothing. She didn't feel even a tingle of power.

Okay, so my orbing is on the fritz, she thought. *I'll have to resort to Plan B. Get home by nonmagical methods.*

Unfortunately, she was halfway across the city from home and she was still wearing her pajamas with monkey faces all over them.

I'm sure Mr. Smelly won't mind if I use the phone, she told herself. The apartment consisted of the small bedroom and an equally small living room/kitchen area. Paige hurried out to the living room, where she found nothing but a futon couch, two milk cartons set up as a coffee table, and a giant flat-screen TV. Clearly Mr. Smelly was a bachelor. She spotted the phone lying on the floor under a magazine.

Paige quickly dialed her home number. As she expected, Piper answered on the first ring.

"Paige?" she demanded.

"In the flesh," Paige replied.

"Why did you orb?" Piper asked. "Where are you? I thought you were sick."

"I *am* sick," Paige said indignantly. "I don't know what happened. One second I was in the kitchen, and the next second I was in my old apartment."

"What?" Piper cried. "Why?"

"I don't know," Paige said. "But some guy lives here now, and he's gonna find me any second, and I can't orb back."

"Wait a minute. Why can't you orb back if you orbed there?"

Take a deep breath, Paige commanded herself. "If I knew the answer to that, I would already be orbing home right now," she said through gritted teeth. "Will you just come get me, please?"

The shower in the other room turned off. Mr. Smelly would be walking out any second.

"I'm on my way," Piper told her. "Meet me out front."

"Yup," Paige said quickly. "I'll be the one in shorty pajamas." She pressed the off button on the phone, gently placed it down on top of the TV, and began tiptoeing toward the front door. So far so good. She reached for the chain lock and slowly, quietly slid the chain off. Now for the dead bolt . . .

As Paige leaned forward to work the lock, her foot landed on a loose board. Too late she remembered that it was the squeaky board.

CREAK!

She grimaced. Then she undid the dead bolt and yanked the door open as fast as she could.

"Hold it!" cried a guy's voice.

Paige took a deep breath and turned to face Mr. Smelly. "I'm really sorry—" The words died in her throat. Before her stood the most gorgeous guy she'd ever seen. Wavy black hair, rippling muscles . . . and a Star Wars towel wrapped around his waist. He held a baseball bat in his hand, apparently ready to do battle even dripping wet and practically naked.

"I thought I heard someone," he said, lowering the bat as he took in Paige's outfit. She patted her hair down, suddenly very aware of how much of a mess she must look.

Mr. Smelly must have been thinking the same thing, because he glanced down at himself and looked almost surprised to find himself wearing nothing but an old towel.

Paige took advantage of his confusion. "I have to go now," she announced. "Buh-bye!"

She fled into the hallway, knowing Mr. Smelly wouldn't be able to follow her far in his towel.

"But I don't get it," Piper said again. "Why would you end up in your old apartment?" She unlocked the front door of the manor and held it open for Paige.

"I was thinking about that on the way home," Paige replied, shuffling inside. "I said I was going back to bed, and then I orbed back to bed. It just wasn't the right bed . . . anymore."

Piper frowned. "That's bizarre."

"You don't have to tell *me*," Paige said.

"Why don't you go back to bed for real this time?" Piper said. "You look awful. I'll check with Leo to see if he has any idea what happened to your orbing."

As Paige headed up the stairs, Piper called to her husband. White light filled the room, and Leo appeared. "What?" he said quickly.

Piper raised an eyebrow. He wasn't usually so brusque. "We have a problem," she said.

"Can you handle it without me?" Leo asked. "I'm in the middle of something."

Piper tried to stay calm. Leo was kind of blowing her off, but she knew that he had a lot of innocents to protect. He wasn't being rude; he was just in a rush to help someone. Still, it was hard not to feel hurt by his impatient tone of voice. "Um, sure. I guess we can figure it out on our own," she said.

"Great. Call if you really need me." Leo vanished without even saying good-bye.

Well, Piper thought, *it's good to know my husband trusts me to deal with problems on my own.* She couldn't help wondering, though, if Leo would still leave her on her own when they had a baby. What if the baby was in trouble and one of Leo's charges needed him? How would he ever be able to choose between those responsibilities?

"I can't think about that right now," Piper murmured. She pulled her cell phone from her bag and dialed Phoebe's cell.

"Hello?" Phoebe answered.

"I need you to come home," Piper told her sister. She plopped onto the overstuffed couch. "Paige is having a magic crisis."

Phoebe groaned. "How bad?"

"Well, I'm not entirely sure yet," Piper said. "She doesn't seem to be in control of her orbing. But maybe it was just a one-time thing."

"I really need to get this psychology assignment done," Phoebe said. "If I get a good grade in this class, the teacher promised me a recommendation guaranteed to get job offers."

"Well, I have a job offer for you right now: being a Charmed One," Piper said. "We need to figure out what's going on with Paige, and Leo's not here—"

"But my assignment is due in class tonight!" Phoebe exclaimed.

"Then the sooner you get here, the sooner we can figure this out and you can finish your assignment and get that high-paying job," Piper stated firmly.

Phoebe sighed. "I'll be there as soon as I can."

There was a little shriek from upstairs. *Paige,* thought Piper. "Listen, Phoebes, I gotta go," she said into the phone. "Hurry home."

Piper hung up and shook her head. Between her two sisters, *someone* always needed help. Piper was usually able to be there for them, but since last night she'd been trying to picture her life with a baby attached. How would she ever find the time to deal with the demands of motherhood on top of Phoebe's needs and Paige's needs?

Paige, she remembered. She jogged up the stairs to check on her sick sister. "Paige?" she called. But there was no answer. "Paige, honey?"

She pushed open the door to Paige's room. It was a mess, as usual, but there was no sign of Paige. "Paige?" Piper called again. She checked the closet and the bathroom. Paige was nowhere to be seen. "Okay, this is officially not funny," Piper muttered. Where was her sister?

Her cell phone rang again, startling her. She clicked it on. "Hello?"

"Help!" cried Paige.

"Hey, lady, hurry up with the phone," whined a kid wearing a Giants baseball cap.

"This is an emergency," Paige told him. She turned away from his smirking face and tried to concentrate on Piper's voice. It wasn't easy, especially since she knew everyone in the huge room was looking at her.

"Where are you?" Piper demanded.

Paige cringed. "In my middle school cafeteria," she replied. She glanced at the circle of giggling preteens gathered behind her in line for the pay phone. "In my pajamas," she added.

"Yikes," Piper said. "Let me guess, you can't orb back?"

"Bingo," Paige replied. She noticed a heavyset, balding man near the cafeteria doors about fifty feet away. "Oh my god, Piper, Mr. Seubert is still here!"

"Who?"

"My seventh-grade health studies teacher," Paige said. "He totally humiliated me once. He made me do an oral report on body odor!"

"Do you think she's a homeless person?" asked one of the girls in line behind her.

"I have to get out of here," Paige said. "Please come get me *now*."

"On my way," Piper said.

Paige hung up the pay phone and turned to the kids. She wished she'd changed out of her pajamas. Or combed her hair. Or brought a box of tissues along. She sneezed. "This is, um, performance art," she told them, and sneezed again.

They all looked at her as if she were crazy. *And they might be right about that,* she thought.

"What's going on over here?" a booming voice called.

"Oh, no. Mr. Seubert," Paige whispered. How was she supposed to explain what she was doing here? She tried to remember any sort of spell to help her hide from him; but the cold medicine was starting to kick in, and she felt too drowsy to think straight. *Why couldn't I at least have orbed back to Mr. O'Leary's fourth-grade class instead?*

The thought wasn't even finished before Paige felt herself orbing. When the white light faded, she found herself scrunched into a tiny desk at the back of an elementary school classroom. The lights were dim, and a film about gorillas was playing on the pull-down screen at the front of the room. Paige glanced around. The two kids sitting on either side of her were fast asleep. No one seemed to have noticed her . . . so far.

"Okay," Paige murmured as she quietly slipped out of the desk. "Here we go again!"

Piper held the steering wheel with one hand and her cell phone with the other. "You're *where*?" she cried.

"At Fisherman's Wharf," Paige said. "Sorry."

Piper pulled the car to the side of the road. Fisherman's Wharf was in the opposite direction from Paige's middle school, the last place she'd called from. "Paige," she said, trying to keep her voice calm, "what are you doing at a tourist trap like that?"

"I don't know." Paige sounded miserable. "The orbing is completely out of control. I just think of something and I orb there."

"Well, why don't you think of the manor and orb back home?"

"It doesn't work!" Paige wailed. "I can't make it work."

Piper put on her blinker and did a U-turn. "Try not to think of *anything* in the next ten minutes then. Otherwise I may never find you."

"How am I supposed to do that?" Paige asked.

"I don't know," Piper said, exasperated. "Meditate or something." She hit the off button and put the cell phone down on the passenger seat. *Maybe I should meditate too,* she thought wryly. *It might calm me down.* So far she'd spent almost the entire day driving around looking for Paige, and it was making her jumpy. And if she was this stressed about taking care of her little sister, she couldn't imagine how she'd be able to handle taking care of a baby!

I have to stop thinking like that, she told herself. *I'm totally overreacting. I'm freaking out about nothing!* She hadn't even been able to buy a pregnancy test yet; she'd been too busy tracking Paige all over town. Piper drove quickly, trying to concentrate on Paige. She felt sorry for her sister; it was bad enough to have a cold, let alone having a cold *and* out of whack powers. This uncontrollable orbing was worse than if Paige's powers had disappeared altogether.

Too bad she's half Whitelighter, Piper thought. *If she didn't have the Whitelighter ability to orb, she wouldn't be bouncing around the city like this.*

Piper gasped as another meaning of that sank in. "It's the Whitelighter blood," she said out loud. "That's what's going on here." She took her foot off the accelerator and pulled to a stop. Her heart was pounding fast. Paige was half Whitelighter and half witch. They'd always known her powers would be different from those of a full witch. But they'd never thought the powers could be dangerous for her.

"Leo!" she called, panicked.

White light filled the car as her husband orbed into the passenger seat. His hair was a mess, and his face was set in a worried expression. Immediately Piper felt stupid for calling him again. He obviously had bigger problems to deal with.

"What's wrong?" Leo asked. He glanced around. "Why are we in the car?"

"I'm going to get Paige," Piper replied. "Her orbing is out of control."

Leo's eyes widened. "Out of control how?"

"She's just orbing all over the place, and she doesn't know why it's happening. Plus, she can't orb when she needs to." Piper narrowed her eyes at him. "Can't you feel it? I thought you could always tell when one of your charges was in trouble."

"I can. But I don't feel anything at all from Paige." He frowned. "Is this why you called me before?"

Piper nodded. "I thought it might be a one-time thing, but I was wrong."

"It's weird that I can't feel anything wrong," Leo said. "So you're saying that Paige doesn't control the orbing, the orbing controls her?"

Piper nodded. "Do you—do you think it's because she's not a full Whitelighter?" she asked, worried. "Maybe as a half Whitelighter, she isn't strong enough to control that kind of power."

Leo shook his head. "No, that's no problem. Paige wouldn't have the power to orb if she weren't strong enough to handle it."

Piper wasn't so sure about that, but she nodded anyway.

"Where's Phoebe?" Leo asked.

"On her way home," Piper told him. "Or maybe she's home by now. I don't know. I've been following Paige around for the past half hour."

"I hope the three of you together can figure this out," Leo said. "Is there anything else? Is Paige in danger?"

"She's in danger of making her cold worse if she doesn't get home soon," Piper said. "But we haven't had any demon sightings or anything. "

"Try to get her home, and I'll investigate what could be causing it as soon as I have time," Leo said. "But I have an innocent in trouble, and I really don't feel any magic crisis from Paige. I don't think there's evil involved here, or I would sense it."

Piper didn't want to worry him anymore, but she couldn't stop thinking about Paige's half-and-half status. "And you're sure her Whitelighter half and her witch half aren't somehow screwing her up?" she asked.

"Honey, no," Leo said. "I don't see what that has to do with it. I need to get back to my innocent—"

"Of course. Go," Piper said, although she didn't want him to.

Leo gave her a smile and a quick kiss. Then he orbed out of the car, leaving Piper alone with her fears for Paige—and for herself. Leo had said this problem had nothing to do with Paige's being the child of a Whitelighter and a witch. But maybe he just didn't want to face that possibility. Because if the union of witch and Whitelighter created a child with power problems, then how could she and Leo ever hope to have a normal baby?

"Where have you been?" cried Phoebe the instant Piper walked in the door. "Where's Paige?"

"I'm here," Paige said with a sniffle, following Piper inside. Phoebe gasped. Paige looked terrible! She was dressed in dirt-smeared pajamas, her hair was a mess, her eyes were bloodshot, and her nose was red.

"Are you okay, sweetie?" Phoebe crooned, brushing Paige's hair off her face.

"No," Paige replied. "I'm taking more cold medicine and going to bed."

"You might want to take a shower too," Piper told her. "And think about sleeping fully clothed."

Paige waved over her shoulder as she trudged upstairs.

Phoebe watched in astonishment as Piper threw herself onto the sofa. "What's going on?" she asked.

"Paige just keeps orbing unexpectedly," Piper answered. "She can't control it."

Phoebe sat down next to Piper. "So I guess it wasn't just a one-time thing."

"Nope."

Phoebe ran through the usual list of threats in her mind. "Do you think there's some demon messing with her?" she asked. "Or maybe a warlock did a spell to steal her orbing power."

Piper shook her head. "Believe me, her orbing power has not been stolen. She's orbed about fifteen times today. She just can't direct it; she can't tell the power where to orb her to."

"Then maybe someone, or something, is confusing her powers to distract us. We'll be so busy trying to deal with Paige's orbing that we won't notice if a demon is up to no good."

Piper shook her head. "Leo didn't think it was evil-related. He can't sense anything wrong."

Well, that's alarming, Phoebe thought. "Do you think maybe there's something wrong with Leo?" she asked.

"No," Piper replied quickly. "I just called him, and he came right away. He was helping an innocent, and he can feel his other charges. He's in total control of his orbing. It's just Paige."

Phoebe didn't like the sound of this. Paige's powers were on the blink and Leo couldn't even tell? That seemed like a pretty big deal. "I'm going to call Cole," she announced.

"Where is he?" Piper asked.

"He's at a homeless shelter, cooking," Phoebe said. "Ever since we vanquished his demon half, he's been trying to spend time volunteering. It's his way of making up for his past evils."

"I've tasted his cooking. He might want to find some other way." Piper smiled. "Don't drag him away from his humanitarian efforts. I'm sure we can solve this on our own. With luck whatever it was has passed. Paige didn't orb once all the way back from Fisherman's Wharf. In fact it's been almost an hour since she had any orbing mishaps at all."

"That could be a good thing, or it could mean it's gotten worse," Phoebe said. "Maybe her orbing power is completely gone now. I think we need to check the Book of Shadows."

"You're pretty gung ho all of a sudden," Piper commented.

"I need to deal with the Paige situation fast so I can get back to my homework," Phoebe said. "I'm really having a hard time with it."

"What is this assignment anyway?" Piper asked.

"My applied psychology class is doing a section on family counseling," Phoebe replied. "We're supposed to write up a treatment plan for a sample case study."

"So they gave you a fake patient and you're supposed to write about how you'd solve its fake problem?" Piper asked.

"Kind of. As a counselor I wouldn't really be trying to *solve* the problem. Somehow I'm supposed to figure out how I would help the patient solve the problem for herself. But my fake patient has a problem I just don't know how to handle."

"What is it?" Piper asked. "Maybe I can help."

"She's a thirty-year-old woman who just had a baby," Phoebe said. "But now that she's a mother, she's totally overwhelmed. It's made her depressed. How am I supposed to help her?"

Piper leaped up from the couch, breathing hard. Phoebe blinked in surprise. "What's wrong?"

"Um . . . maybe you *should* go check the Book of Shadows about Paige," Piper said. "I, uh, I have to go." Then she ran out of the living room.

Phoebe stared after her for a moment, baffled. "I need someone sane," she murmured, picking up the phone to call Cole.

...

"You *like* babies," Piper told the reflection in the mirror over her dresser. "You're happy about having a baby with Leo." Frustrated, she turned away from her reflection and fell face-down on the bed. It was true she and Leo did want a family. They'd talked about it over and over, how their kids would have his light hair and her brown eyes. How much fun it would be to discover their magical powers as they grew. How complete it would make them both feel. So why was she freaking out about it now that it was really happening?

Memories of her own mother flooded her. Patty had always been so competent, even with three daughters to take care of. Piper could picture her now, helping Prue with her homework, teaching Piper to tie her shoes, and feeding baby Phoebe all at the same time. *Will I ever be able to juggle so many things at once?* Piper wondered. She couldn't even find a way to help Phoebe with her homework and solve Paige's orbing problem.

Plus, her baby was going to be like Paige, half Whitelighter and half witch. "And all out of control," Piper murmured. After an entire day of chasing Paige around, she was exhausted. How much worse would it be with a five-year-old?

The phone rang. Piper groaned. "Please don't let this be Paige," she muttered. If Paige had started surprise orbing again, who knew where she might be? Piper picked up the receiver on the bedside table. "Hello?"

"Hi, Ms. Halliwell?" A man's voice answered her. "This is Gerry, with Maxells Contractors."

"Yes. Mr., uh, Gerry," Piper said. "What can I do for you?"

"We have a problem with the bathroom at your club," Gerry told her.

Of course you have a problem, Piper thought. *Everyone I talk to today has a problem.* "Define *problem,*" she said.

"Well, while we were demolishing the wall, we hit a sewage pipe," Gerry told her. "It burst, and you've got water everywhere. And some sewage."

"Ewww," Piper moaned.

"Yeah, it's a pretty big mess," he said.

At least it's not a magical mess, Piper thought. *Those are harder to fix.*

"We're not a cleanup crew, Ms. Halliwell." Gerry went on. "We're construction. You're gonna have to get another crew in here."

"What?" Piper cried. "But you're the ones who broke the pipe!"

"I know, but we don't clean," he replied.

"Hiring another crew will cost me twice as much," Piper told him. "This is completely wrong."

"You can take that up with the union," Gerry said. "But you might want to come down and check it out first."

"Fine," Piper said. "I'll be right there."

Paige finished towel-drying her hair and headed back into her bedroom. "Finally, I can sleep off this cold," she murmured. She'd had a nice, steamy shower, a little plastic cup full of cold medicine, and a big glass of water. She was starting to feel like a new woman.

A familiar tingling sensation began in her fingers. "Oh, no," she groaned. "Not again!"

She orbed into the living room. Phoebe and Cole looked up in surprise as she suddenly appeared on the couch.

"Whew!" Paige said. "I was afraid I was going to end up in some public place again without being dressed." She glanced down at her fuzzy chenille bathrobe. "In fact I think I'll go put on some regular clothes just in case."

"How are you doing?" Cole asked. "Phoebe just filled me in on your orbing issues."

Paige shrugged. "I don't feel any other magical weirdness. I just keep orbing. How about you guys?"

"You're the only one with power problems," Phoebe told her. "I just have writer's block." Phoebe began typing on her laptop, then stopped, sighed, and hit delete.

"I know that's due tonight, but if we don't do something to help Paige first, there may be bigger problems than turning in your homework on time," Cole said.

"Leo said it's not demonic," Phoebe answered.

"That doesn't mean we can ignore it," Cole said. "Paige can't keep bouncing around all day."

Paige shot him a smile. She didn't always trust Cole, but it was nice of him to be worried for her. "I think this orbing problem might just be a symptom of my cold. Like magic hiccups," she told him.

"But you've had colds before and they never affected your powers," Cole said.

Paige thought about that. He had a point. She was still so new at being a Charmed One that she never knew what might affect her powers.

"Well, at least I haven't encountered any demons," Paige said. "And I've been all over the city."

"But I won't be satisfied until I know what's causing it," Cole said. "Let's do this: I'll check the Book of Shadows. Paige, you get some sleep. And Phoebe can scry for demons and then finish her assignment."

Paige hesitated. She knew that Cole wasn't a demon anymore and that he was good now. But the idea of him alone in the attic with the Book of Shadows made her nervous. Maybe when he and Phoebe had been married for ten years or so, Paige would start to relax around him. But not now.

"Actually I'd like to help," she announced. "The cold medicine is kicking in. I'll just get dressed, and then I'll help you look through the Book of Shadows."

"Okay," Cole said. "I'll meet you in the attic."

Paige shot Phoebe a worried glance. She didn't want to offend her sister by being so mistrustful of her fiancé. But Phoebe was staring at her computer, concentrating deeply but not typing a single word. She probably hadn't even heard half of the conversation between Cole and Paige.

Paige turned toward the stairs, already picturing the clothes she wanted to wear. A nice warm tracksuit was the perfect thing to keep her toasty while she was sick. *I wish I could take a nap*. She thought longingly of her bed with the deep blue Indian print bedspread and the small jade Buddha on her bedside table. . . .

Something hard and cold landed in Paige's hand. "Whoa!" she cried, opening her eyes. In her hand was the Buddha statue from her bedroom. She gaped at it.

"What happened?" Cole asked. Even Phoebe was paying attention now.

"Um, I guess I orbed the Buddha from upstairs," Paige said. "I was thinking about it, and suddenly there it was."

"But you didn't call for it," Phoebe said.

"I know." Paige chewed on her lip. "Do you think this is another new example of my powers acting up?"

"Could be," Cole said. "And the sooner we find out who's causing it, the sooner we can stop it." He headed for the stairs. Paige hesitated only long enough to place the Buddha on the coffee table. Then she ran after Cole.

"How did the pipe break?" Piper demanded. She couldn't believe the mess in P3. The flood from the bathroom had spread out to the main area, and Piper was afraid it might damage the wooden dance floor.

Gerry and his two assistants sat on stools at the bar. They weren't terribly upset. "Billy here hit it with an ax," Gerry said.

"Then this is totally your fault!" Piper yelled. "You're responsible for fixing it!"

"The schematics you gave us didn't show any pipes in that wall," Gerry told her. He unwrapped a stick of gum and shoved it into his mouth. Then he smiled at Piper as if he had not a care in the world.

She thought she might explode. Some relaxing week off. She needed a moment to think. She waved her hand to freeze the three men.

Gerry continued chewing his gum agreeably. Piper stared at him in astonishment.

"What?" he asked, noticing her expression. He glanced at his two assistants, both of whom were frozen in place. "Oh."

Lightning-fast, he jumped out of his seat and vaulted over the bar.

Well, this can't be good, Piper thought to herself. "Why aren't you frozen?" she cried.

"Uh, I'm a demon," he said from behind the bar. "A Farza demon. We can't be frozen. In fact that's pretty much our only power."

"A *demon?*" Piper cried. "I hired a demon to redo my bathroom?" She strode to the bar and peered over it at Gerry. Now she noticed a faint purple glow around his eyes. "This is just perfect after the day I've had."

Gerry gave a little whimper. "Look, I just needed the money. I didn't know you were a witch." His hair was standing on end, making him look like a frightened troll doll. "We're pacifist demons," he said. "We're good guys!"

"Good demons?" Piper asked. "There's no such thing."

"Well, okay, so we're not exactly *good*. We're . . . neutral," Gerry said, his hair relaxing a bit. "We're like Switzerland. We mostly just hide."

"Switzerland doesn't hide," Piper said.

Gerry's hair stood straight up again. "Are you gonna vanquish me?" he asked, cringing.

Piper thought about it. "Maybe," she said. She frowned. "Let me get this straight. You're actually a contractor?" Gerry nodded. "You're not here to fight me?" Piper held up her hand, ready to explode him.

"No! I told you, I didn't even know you were a witch!" Gerry yelped. "I never would've taken this job if I knew."

She kept her hand up. "What are you after?" she asked. "Who sent you?"

"No one," he answered. "I needed the job. I can't do magic. I have to work like a mortal to put food on the table."

Piper held his gaze for a moment, then lowered her hand. He was so pathetic that she almost felt sorry for him. But demons could never be trusted. They lied like, well, demons.

"Sorry about the sewage pipe," Gerry told her. "I know a guy who can clean it up cheap."

Piper narrowed her eyes. "You're fired," she said.

"Look for a spell to reveal an unseen enemy," Cole said.

Paige blew her nose and tossed the tissue onto the pile at her feet. "The dust up here is making my congestion worse," she said. The Halliwell attic wasn't *quite* as messy as a typical attic, mostly because Piper was a neat freak. But Paige's head hurt, and she felt like whining a little bit.

Cole was frustrated, she could tell. They had been trying to figure out what was wrong with her powers for almost two hours now. She'd accidentally orbed twice, but luckily both times she'd ended up within walking distance of the manor.

"Why don't you go take a nap?" Cole asked. "I'll keep working on this."

Paige met his challenging eyes. He was practically daring her to trust him up here with the book, the source of the Charmed Ones' power. *My sister's future husband or not, he'll always be a demon to me,* she realized. "It's okay," she said. "I'll stay and help. After all, it's my magic that's at stake."

Cole shook his head. "Fine. So we've ruled out demons of the first order. Try to find that reveal spell."

Paige carefully turned the parchment pages of the old book. She loved the Book of Shadows. The first time she'd touched it, she could feel the power radiating from it and surrounding her. She'd felt at home in this house from that moment on. *I've got to get my powers under control,* she thought. *Book of Shadows, all you Halliwell witches before me, help me discover what's happening.*

There was a whoosh of air through the room, and the pages of the book blew in the wind. Paige looked down to find it open to a reveal spell, the exact one she needed. She smiled. "Thanks," she whispered to the book.

"Did you find it?" Cole asked, hurrying to her side.

"Sure did," Paige replied. "Now all we need to do is—aaagh!" Paige felt herself begin to orb. *Not now,* she thought frantically. She grabbed the podium that held the Book of Shadows and dug her fingers into the wood. But it was no use. She was orbing again, against her will.

And who knew where she'd end up?

"What do you mean you lost her?" Piper cried. "Where did she go?"

Cole shrugged. "We were about to do a reveal spell to show us who's causing her orbing problems," he answered. "And then she orbed. It's not like I can follow her anymore."

Piper realized she shouldn't have left the manor when Paige was in trouble, but she'd had no choice. Besides, she'd left Phoebe and Cole there. Both alleged responsible adults. Why did she always have to be the mom? She'd be a mom to someone soon enough probably. And to someone who could have the same problems Paige was experiencing now. When that happened, she wouldn't be able just to run down to P3 when someone called. She'd have to find some other way to handle the dual responsibilities of career and family.

Piper forced herself to sit still. She had to stop overreacting this way; it wasn't helping anyone.

"Paige will call and tell us where she is," Phoebe said. "Stop pacing, Cole."

"Yeah," Piper said. "You're going to wear out the carpet." He'd been pacing when she got home from P3 five minutes ago, and he kept pacing now.

"It's my fault," he said. "I should have been able to stop her from orbing."

"Cole, even Phoebe and I couldn't stop her," Piper told him. "It's not your fault." *It's just Paige's half-and-half nature,* she added silently.

"But what if she orbed into a trap?" Cole asked. "We were just about to say the reveal spell. Maybe when she thought about doing it, her powers orbed her straight to the people she was trying to reveal. Isn't that the way it's been working?"

Phoebe shot Piper a panicked look. "That kind of makes sense," she said. "Paige could be surrounded by demons right now."

"I don't think so," Piper said. "Leo would've sensed it if Paige's problem was being caused by demons."

"Where is Leo anyway?" Phoebe asked. "Shouldn't he be here to help Paige?"

Piper felt a rush of annoyance at her husband. He *should* be here. This was a problem that could eventually affect their own child. Immediately she was consumed by guilt for being so disloyal. Leo would be here if he could. "One of his other charges had a major crisis," she said. "He'll be back soon."

"We don't even know where she is," Cole said. "This could get serious before then."

"I just don't think there's a demon involved," Piper told him. "I think this problem is coming from Paige herself. Because she's—she's not one thing or the other." Piper picked up a throw pillow from the couch and hugged it to her chest. She was afraid to meet Phoebe's eyes. Saying this out loud made it all seem horribly real. "I think this is happening because Paige is half Whitelighter and half witch." She went on. "Her powers are still evolving. You know how our powers have changed over time. Well, Paige's powers are changing too. Only she can't control them, because she's just a half witch. And she can't control the Whitelighter powers either because she's only a half Whitelighter."

Piper's voice broke, and she looked up at her sister. "What if Paige is going to be like this forever?" she whispered. "Because she inherited powers she can't handle."

Phoebe shook her head. "I don't think so," she said skeptically. "She's a Charmed One after all. She's strong. I think something is messing with Paige's powers."

"So do I," Cole said.

Piper didn't know what to say. Her sister and brother-in-law were practically dismissing her deepest, darkest fears!

Maybe they're right, she thought hopefully. *Maybe I'm just making this whole thing up.* "Do you really think she might be wherever the reveal spell would've sent her?" Piper asked Cole.

"There's only one way to find out," he replied.

• • •

"A drugstore," Paige said, looking around at the shelves of medicines. "Didn't see that coming." Had she been talking to Cole about a drugstore right before she orbed? She didn't think so. She headed outside so she could figure out where in San Francisco she was. At least she *hoped* she was still in San Francisco!

In front of the store was a pay phone. Paige walked toward it; she needed to call home. *If this keeps up, I'm going to have to chain my cell phone to my wrist,* she thought.

A cell phone with a hot pink zebra-striped faceplate appeared in her hand. Paige looked at it in surprise. She had obviously orbed it from some innocent stranger! "Weird," she said. But she needed to use it. She dialed the number of the manor.

Piper answered on the first ring. "Where are you?"

"At a drugstore in the Haight," Paige said. "And I'm calling you from a cell phone that just appeared in my hand out of nowhere."

"You stole someone's phone?" Piper asked.

"No!" Paige replied. "Well, not on purpose." Her voice trailed off as she noticed a middle-aged blond woman staring at her. *Staring at the cell phone is more like it,* Paige thought. "I gotta go," she told her sister.

"Wait, Paige—" Piper started to answer her, but Paige hit the off button.

The blond woman approached her. "Excuse me," she said sharply. "But I believe that's my phone. It just flew out of my hand a minute ago." She eyed Paige suspiciously.

"Um, yeah." Paige tried to think of an excuse. "I found it on the sidewalk."

Not buying Paige's story, the woman frowned and held out her hand. Paige gave her the phone and turned away. *How embarrassing,* she thought. *I'm a magical shoplifter.*

She glanced around, trying to figure out how to get home now that she'd been disconnected from Piper. Her sister had done enough driving around after her for one day. She'd just find her own way home. She approached a teenage guy standing on the street corner. "Hi," Paige said. "I'm kind of lost. Do you have any idea what the bus schedules are around here?"

There was a whoosh of power, and three bus schedules appeared in Paige's hand. The teenager looked confused, and Paige hastily shoved the papers into the pocket of her track pants. She pasted an innocent smile on her face. "Uh, I think they run every fifteen minutes or so," the teen said.

"Thanks." Paige headed toward a bench near the bus stop sign. She was still drowsy from the cold medicine and wanted to sit down. *It's a good thing I didn't ask him for the time,* she thought. *I would've ended up stealing someone's watch by accident!*

As she lowered herself onto the bench, she felt a cool, heavy band around her wrist. Sure enough, a man's gold watch had orbed onto Paige's wrist.

Oh, no, she thought. *Me and my big mouth!* She glanced around the crowd, watching for signs of someone realizing his watch was gone. Her power of telekinesis orbed objects to her when she called for them, but usually they were objects that she could see to begin with. Right now things seemed to be orbing into her hands from all different places. And she wasn't even trying to call them.

Paige knew she needed to get home and stay there until she and her sisters could figure out what was causing this. Maybe they could do some kind of binding spell to keep her in one place. When a bus pulled up to the stop, Paige climbed on board and scanned for a seat. There was only one available, next to a harried-looking woman with about three shopping bags full of toys. One of the bags sat on the empty seat.

"Could I please sit here?" Paige asked.

The woman ignored her.

"Excuse me?" Paige raised her voice so she could be heard over the roar of the bus's engine. "Could you move the shopping bag so I can sit?"

Paige jumped in surprise as a shopping bag full of men's clothing appeared in her hands. That finally got the woman's attention—and everyone else's.

"Hey!" yelled a tall Latino from the front of the bus. "That's my bag!" He jumped up and strode toward Paige. "Give it back!"

Paige held out the shopping bag. "No problem," she said. How could she explain to him what had just happened? Everyone on the bus was watching her suspiciously. "Um . . . ," she said lamely. Nothing came to her.

The guy snatched the bag from her hand. "I think you should get off this bus," he told her. "Nobody wants a thief on board." Looking around, Paige had a feeling he was right.

The bus pulled over to the curb, and the driver flung open the doors. "This is your stop," he said gruffly.

Quietly Paige made her way out the doors, feeling lonelier than she ever had in her life.

"She said she was in the Haight, but she didn't say where," Piper said. "Should I go look for her?"

"I think we should finish the reveal spell and find out who's causing all this," Phoebe replied. "That's the only way we can really help Paige." She headed for the stairs, Cole at her heels. Piper sighed. She still didn't think there was a demon after Paige, but she'd been outvoted.

She had a feeling that the others just didn't *want* to believe her. They didn't want to face the possibility that Paige might be like this forever. That she'd been ruined by her witch/Whitelighter ancestry. The way Piper's baby might be ruined.

Piper sighed. The Elders had fought hard to keep her and Leo from marrying. Could this be the reason? It would have been nice to have known in advance.

I need to focus on Paige, she thought. Her sister was in trouble right now. Maybe by the time she had this baby, they would have found a solution to the problem. She slowly climbed the stairs and joined Phoebe and Cole in the attic. "Let's call Leo," she said.

"Fine with me," Phoebe replied. "We can use the help. The sooner we take care of this, the sooner I can get back to . . . not doing my class assignment."

Piper exchanged a smile with Cole. They both knew Phoebe would get over her writer's block and meet her deadline—as long as nothing magical interfered.

"Leo!" Piper called. Nothing happened.

"Leo?" Phoebe tried. Still nothing.

Piper's heart leaped into her throat. Why wasn't he answering? Not only was it his duty as a Whitelighter to come when they needed him, but it was his duty as her husband! "Do you think he's hurt?" she asked, trying to keep her voice from trembling. "Maybe this has something to do with why he couldn't sense Paige's orbing problems."

Phoebe rushed over and put her arm around Piper's shoulders. "You said he had an innocent in danger this morning, right?"

Piper nodded.

"Then he's probably busy protecting her right now," Cole said.

"Right," Phoebe said. "He'll be here as soon as he can."

But Piper noticed the troubled expressions on their faces. They were worried about Leo too. Piper felt a little dizzy as concern for her husband's safety threatened to overwhelm her. She took a deep breath and pushed down her fears.

"Let's do the reveal spell," she said. She walked straight over to the Book of Shadows. It was already open to the right page. "To reveal an unseen enemy," she read. "That sounds about right."

Phoebe rushed to her side. Together they read the incantation:

Unseen, unknown though he be,
He shall be revealed to me.
All the elements, you we ask.
Let our enemy be unmasked.

A rush of magic filled the air of the attic. But before the spell could work, Piper heard her cell phone ringing downstairs. She abandoned the spell and ran for it. It could be Paige, calling for someone to pick her up. Or it could be Leo, telling her that he was okay.

She pulled the phone from her bag and answered just before the call went to voice mail. "Hello?" she said breathlessly.

"Piper Halliwell?" a stern voice asked.

"Yes."

"This is Sergeant Engler with the SFPD. We have your sister, Paige Matthews."

"But I didn't steal anything," Paige insisted to the heavyset cop walking her toward a holding cell. "It's all a big misunderstanding."

The woman grunted in reply. "Sure it is, sweetheart," she said sarcastically. "No one in here ever does anything wrong."

"No, I do things wrong all the time," Paige replied. "What I mean is, I don't do illegal wrong things, but my sisters are always telling me to—"

The officer couldn't care less. She opened the door of the holding cell, and gestured to Paige to enter. Once Paige was safely inside, the woman closed and locked the door, then left without even a glance at Paige.

"—be more careful." Paige finally finished her sentence.

An African American girl about Paige's age sat on one of the benches. Paige took a seat on the other one. "So what are you in for?" she asked the girl.

The girl looked nervous. "They pulled me over for speeding and found out about all my unpaid parking tickets," she said. "I guess they're allowed to arrest you for that after a while."

Paige's mouth dropped open. "You're in jail for *parking*?"

The girl cracked a smile. "Pretty stupid, huh? I get home from work so late, there's never any legal parking left on my block. I never paid them. I thought I was protesting the system."

Paige nodded.

"How about you?" the girl asked.

"Um, shoplifting," Paige said. "They think I stole a pair of sunglasses from a sidewalk vendor."

"Did you?"

"Technically, yes," Paige replied. "But I didn't mean to. They're not even cool glasses; they have that extreme sports wraparound thing going on."

The girl wrinkled her nose.

"Exactly," Paige said. "But the sun was hurting my eyes, so I said I needed sunglasses. . . ." Her voice trailed off. She couldn't tell this girl the truth: She'd gone up to the sunglass cart and said she needed shades. Then, before she could even move to point to a pair she wanted, the ugly sports shades had orbed right onto her face. The vendor had freaked out and accused her of taking them. Paige didn't have much of a leg to stand on. "My orbing is on the blink today" wasn't an excuse that most people would buy.

"Anyway," she said, "why would I steal glasses I don't want?"

The girl grinned.

"I hope my sister gets here soon," Paige went on. "I have a bad cold. I need some herbal tea." She jumped as a teacup filled with hot liquid appeared in her hand. *Uh-oh,* she thought. *How am I going to explain this one?* She slowly raised her eyes to the girl, who was staring back openmouthed.

"I bet they'll think I shoplifted this tea too!" Paige said, trying to lighten the mood.

The girl continued to stare at her, speechless.

Might as well drink it, Paige thought, *since I guess our conversation is over.* Luckily, most mortals tended to ignore anything they couldn't explain, so Paige simply lifted the teacup to her lips—and orbed.

"Piper!" Phoebe called after her sister. But it was no use. Piper had run off to answer the phone as they were reciting the reveal spell. The magic wind still blew through the attic. Phoebe concentrated on the spell. "Let our enemy be unmasked," she said again.

A form appeared in the air before her. At first it was just a shimmering light. Then it grew stronger, taking on a rectangular shape that looked familiar.

"It's a door!" Phoebe cried. Cole came over to stand in front of her, just in case something evil decided to come through the door.

The rectangle of light grew brighter and brighter, forcing Phoebe to hold her hand up to block the glare. Then a shadow passed through the light.

"There's something inside," she whispered to Cole.

"Your hidden enemy," he replied.

Phoebe squinted into the light. "I can't see who it is," she said, frustrated. She stepped closer to the light just as the shadowy form inside came flying out as if someone had pushed an ejector button. He collided with Phoebe, and they both went down.

Phoebe's martial arts training kicked in, and she flipped herself back onto her feet in a split second. Instinctively she dropped into a fighting stance. So did the guy from the door of light. As they stood ready, the magic door popped out of existence, leaving the attic in its usual afternoon dimness. Lights swam before Phoebe's eyes; she could barely see the demon in front of her. All she could make out was a faint purple glow and some seriously bad hair.

"Who are you?" she demanded.

She heard the floorboards creak as Cole crept around behind the guy.

"Speak up!" she yelled. "Who are you?"

"Gerry McDonald," the guy said. "Who are you?"

Phoebe's eyes were slowly returning to normal, and now she could see that the demon was dressed in filthy overalls and work boots. He looked just like a normal man, except for the purple glow around his eyes and the troll-like hair that stood straight up on his head. "How did I get here?" he asked.

"I did a spell," Phoebe said, "to show my enemy."

Gerry's hair puffed up even more. "Oh, man, you're a witch?" he whined. "What is it with me and witches today?"

"What kind of demon are you?" Phoebe asked, still in her fighting stance.

"The totally useless kind," Gerry responded in a defeated tone. "I'm a terrible fighter, you know. I'm from a race of pacifist demons. I'm not even going to try to take you on." He held up his hands in surrender.

"You're a Farza demon?" Cole asked.

Gerry nodded glumly, his hair still on end like a frightened cat's.

"It's true, they're cowards," Cole told Phoebe.

"Pacifists," Gerry said, correcting him. He glanced at Phoebe. "Either way, no threat to you."

Phoebe didn't relax. "What have you done to my sister's powers?" she asked.

Gerry laughed. "Lady, I don't even know your sister. I don't know *you*."

This was exasperating. Phoebe glanced over Gerry's shoulder at Cole. "This is obviously going to take awhile," she said. "Why don't you tie him up?"

"Come on, that's not necessary," Gerry said. But he didn't fight as Cole secured him to a chair. And his hair started to relax a little.

Phoebe pulled her fiancé out into the stairwell so they could talk without the demon hearing them. "He's trying to stall," Phoebe said. "That means Paige might be in danger somewhere. Maybe he has an accomplice working on taking her powers. Maybe they even have her hostage somewhere."

"Farzas really are cowards," Cole said. "They barely even count as demons. They don't have any true powers."

"Well, that doesn't mean he isn't friends with evil demons or warlocks," she told him.

"Okay, you stay here and work on him," Cole said. "I'll try to find Paige."

"What about Piper?" Phoebe asked, worried. "Do you think that phone call was important?"

Cole shrugged. "I think she's probably out looking for Leo. With luck she'll find him, and they'll both come back to help us."

I cannot believe I'm bailing my sister out of jail. Piper was fuming as she pulled into a parking space at the police station. *Of all the irresponsible, juvenile things to do . . .*

Paige had been caught shoplifting; at least that's what the police had said on the phone. Piper tried to calm down as she walked into the building. It was probably another power mixup. Paige wouldn't really steal something. But it was still humiliating to have to pick her up in jail.

It was bad enough to have a sister in this sort of trouble. Piper couldn't even imagine how she'd feel as the *mother* of a magical juvenile delinquent.

"I'm here to pay bail for Paige Matthews," she told the officer at the desk. She handed him the cash she'd stopped to get on the way.

"This will take a few minutes to process," he was saying when a woman's scream cut him off.

Instantly police officers were running in all directions. Piper ducked below the counter until the hubbub died down. "What happened?" she asked the cop on duty.

He looked at her suspiciously. "Did you say you were here for Paige Matthews?" he asked.

Piper nodded.

"Well, she's gone," he said. "Just vanished out of the holding cell, according to her cell mate." He nodded toward a pretty African American girl seated at a desk and surrounded by cops.

The girl looked terrified. "Poof!" she was saying. "She just . . . disappeared."

Oh, no, Piper thought. *Paige's unplanned orbing strikes again.*

The officer was still watching Piper closely. "You gonna 'poof' too?" he asked.

"If only. Well, you have the bail money," Piper told him. "I guess my sister found her own way home." She gave him a little wave and got out of there as fast as possible.

Her cell phone started ringing before she even got back to the car. "Paige?" she answered.

"Yeah. Did you get to the police station yet?"

Piper climbed into the driver's seat. "Yup. Just in time to hear you orb out of there. I think your cell mate is going to need therapy to get over this."

Paige groaned. "I wish I knew how to stop it from happening," she said. "I'm getting really tired of orbing around like this."

Piper tried to ignore her feelings of concern. If she was right about what she suspected was causing this whole thing, then Paige was going to be orbing around this way for the rest of her life. "Where are you?" she asked.

"On a BART train," Paige replied. "I cleared the entire car when I appeared out of thin air. It's kinda comfy having it all to myself."

Piper chuckled. "I'll bet."

"I'll take the train home," Paige said.

"Okay. Call if you orb somewhere else," Piper told her before hanging up. Then she dropped her head to the steering wheel and closed her eyes. All the day's pressures, real and self-imposed, were getting the better of her. It was bad enough being on constant red alert against demons and other unspeakable evil. But when you added unpredictable powers into the mix, there was no respite in sight. Plus, she was worried about her husband. It wasn't like him not to come when she called. She fluctuated between feeling angry that he wasn't here to help and worried that something terrible had happened. She'd assumed that she could depend on Leo to share the burdens of parenthood, but today's events made it clear that sometimes he just wouldn't be able to be there. Piper felt a tear make its way slowly down her cheek.

Imbolc is a day to celebrate the return of life, a voice inside her head whispered. *Even in the darkest night of winter, life still remains. The sun will come again and bring with it new life and new happiness.*

Piper lifted her head and wiped away the tear. She'd forgotten all about Imbolc. But maybe the day had a message for her. Even though things looked bad now, it could, and would, get better.

The phone rang, and Piper snatched it up.

"Piper, help," Paige cried. "I just accidentally orbed a famous painting into my hands. Now I'm an art thief!"

Piper sighed. *So much for things getting better*.

"I don't know what you're talking about," Gerry said for the tenth time. "I've never heard of the Charmed Ones."

"What? You don't get the *Demon Daily News*? Every demon's heard of the Charmed Ones," Phoebe told him.

"I told you, I'm not much of a demon," Gerry said. "I try to avoid confrontation, and that means avoiding other demons."

Phoebe rubbed her temples. They'd been having the same conversation over and over again ever since Cole left. She was actually starting to believe that this demon wasn't involved with Paige's power mishaps. "You've never heard of Paige Matthews," she said.

"No."

"Okay, what about me? Phoebe Halliwell?"

Gerry's eyes widened, increasing their purple glow. "Halliwell?" he repeated. "As in Piper Halliwell?"

"Yes," she said. "What do you know about Piper?"

"That she's a dragon lady," Gerry said. "She fired me this morning for something that was totally not my fault."

Phoebe could feel her mouth hanging open. "She *fired* you? What exactly had she *hired* you to do in the first place?" Many different scenarios, all of them bad, filled her head. Why would Piper be hiring demons? The only thing she should be doing with demons was vanquishing them. Maybe Piper wasn't really

Piper. Maybe her body had been taken over by a warlock. She *had* been acting kind of strange today. . . .

"She hired me to expand the bathroom in her nightclub," Gerry said. "But then a pipe burst—"

"Hold on a minute." Phoebe interrupted him. "*You're* the contractor?"

"Yeah," he said. "What is it with you witches? Haven't you ever heard of a down-on-his-luck demon before?"

Phoebe frowned. "No," she said. She threw herself down onto one of the old chairs and tried to think things through. Paige's powers were going crazy. Piper had hired a demon to redo P3. Leo was MIA. *And my family counseling assignment still isn't done,* she remembered miserably.

"I don't know whether I can trust you or not," she said. "So we're just going to have to wait for Piper to come home." She ignored Gerry's groan. "And no more noise out of you!" she added. "I have to work."

She pulled her computer onto her lap and opened the file with her half-finished treatment plan for her fake patient. She stared at the screen. She couldn't think of a single thing to write.

"You want some help?" asked Gerry.

"What am I supposed to do with this painting?" Paige asked, gazing down at the still life on her lap. It was a small, beautiful piece by one of her favorite artists from New York.

"Hide it," Piper said, her eyes on the road. "And when Leo turns up again, we'll have him orb it back to the gallery."

"I don't even know what gallery it came from," Paige said miserably. "I was just sitting on the train, minding my own business. All I did was think about how I used to like *painting* when I was a kid, and suddenly there it was."

"You need to stop thinking," Piper told her.

Both sisters cracked up.

"Thanks for the advice," Paige said. "At this rate, I barely have *time* to think anyway. If I'm not orbing around with no warning, I'm busy orbing objects in from who knows where."

Piper just chewed on her lip and concentrated on driving. Paige didn't know what to make of it. Usually her oldest sister was the one who took care of them all, the one who always had a plan of action. But today Piper seemed distracted.

"Where's Leo?" Paige asked.

"I'm not sure," Piper told her. "He was helping an innocent in danger, and he didn't come when Phoebe and I called him."

"Wow, that's unusual," Paige said. *That explains the distraction factor,* she thought.

"Paige, can I ask you a question?" Piper said. "Is this the first time you've felt your powers were too much for you?"

O-kay, abrupt change of subject, Paige thought. Piper must be more worried about Leo than she wanted to admit. "I don't feel like they're too much for me," she replied. "I just feel like I can't control them right now."

"It's the same thing, isn't it?" Piper asked. "You can't control them, it means they're too strong for you."

Paige hesitated. That almost seemed like an insult. "Do you mean this has never happened to you?" she asked. "Or to Phoebe or Prue? None of you ever lost control of your powers temporarily?"

"Well, I guess that's happened," Piper said. "But you're different. None of us are half Whitelighter."

"Why does that matter?" Paige asked. Now she was beginning to feel frightened. She'd assumed this wacky power stuff was fairly normal or at least would eventually be explained away.

"I just wonder if we've been training you wrong or if our focus has been misdirected," Piper said. "We only know about witch things. Maybe Leo should help you learn more about your Whitelighter powers when he gets back."

"Maybe," Paige said quietly. But she wasn't quite sure what Piper was getting at, and she wasn't quite sure she really wanted to know.

"Up here!" Phoebe called down the stairs to Piper and Paige after she saw the SUV parked in the driveway. She was in a good mood because she'd finally finished her assignment with Gerry's help. She'd simply talked it over with him. And talking it through helped her find the thread she'd been looking for to tie her thoughts together. After that, writing it up was a snap. She was finishing the last paragraph when Piper and Paige walked into the attic.

As Phoebe expected, Piper was less than thrilled to see Gerry there. She took one look at him and grabbed Phoebe by the arm. "Let's go *downstairs* where the demon can't hear us," she said through gritted teeth.

Phoebe followed her to the bottom of the main staircase while Paige sat on the last step and leaned her head against the banister.

"What is he doing here?" Piper demanded.

"The reveal spell found him," Phoebe told her. "Where have you been, by the way? Both of you?"

"I had to go bail Paige out of jail," Piper snapped. Phoebe and Paige exchanged a look.

"It's a long story," Paige said. "I hope I can tell it to you without orbing in the middle."

Piper's forehead wrinkled as she digested the information Phoebe had just related. "Wait a minute," she said. "You think Gerry the demon is responsible for Paige's power issues?"

"That's what the spell said," Phoebe answered with a shrug.

"He told me he didn't have any powers!" Piper cried.

"Well, Cole did say that Farza demons aren't all that evil. And Gerry seems pretty harmless. Plus, he came up with lots of good stuff for my psychology assignment."

"The *demon* did?" Paige asked.

"He's had a hard life," Phoebe said. "Everyone wants to fight with demons, but all he wants to do is avoid violence. That kind of thing makes people compassionate."

"Tell me about it," Paige said. "Some of the most giving people I meet at Social Services are the ones with the most difficult lives."

"Hello?" Piper cried. "There's a demon upstairs! I don't care how compassionate he is, we need to get rid of him."

"Why is he messing with my powers?" Paige asked.

"I'm not sure," Phoebe said. "He says he isn't. He doesn't even know who you are. Plus, he doesn't have any powers of his own, so I don't know how he could be doing this to you."

"But the reveal spell showed us Gerry," Piper said.

Phoebe didn't know what to think. She had to admit that now she kind of liked Gerry. "We asked the spell to show us our enemy. How is Gerry our enemy?"

Piper gasped. "I can't believe this!"

"What?"

"He's *my* enemy," she said. "I was doing the spell with you, so it sent my enemy. He and his guys completely screwed up at P3 today. The place is a mess! I was so mad at him that I fired him. So at the time we did the spell, he was my biggest 'enemy.'"

"You mean he's not causing my powers to go crazy?" Paige asked.

"Sorry." Piper gave Paige an apologetic smile. "I don't think so. We'd better do a truth spell on him just to make sure."

"Do you guys need me?" Paige asked. "I want to take a nap; all this orbing is wearing me out. You don't think I can orb while I'm asleep, do you?"

"Yikes, I hope not!" Phoebe felt helpless. Poor Paige was sick and exhausted, and so far they hadn't been able to help her at all. "But we'll come check on you every ten minutes to make sure you're still there."

"Thanks." Paige shuffled off toward the bathroom.

"Okay, lady," Phoebe told her older sister. "Let's go do a truth spell!"

They headed back into the attic, and Phoebe located a simple spell near the front of the Book of Shadows. Piper looked over her shoulder as they read:

Powers that be, join with me
To show the truth for all to see.

Piper said the words along with Phoebe, but Phoebe could feel that her concentration was wavering. *She can't stop worrying about Paige and Leo,* Phoebe realized. She just hoped Piper's distraction wouldn't weaken the Charmed Ones' power.

Gerry sat in the chair in front of them, watching with interest. As the incantation ended, Phoebe felt the familiar whoosh of power fill the attic air.

"Am I supposed to feel different?" Gerry asked.

"I don't know," Piper replied. "Do you?"

"Not really."

"Tell us the truth," Phoebe said to him. "Have you been using magic to disrupt our sister's powers?"

"No," Gerry said. "But I did lie to Piper."

"What?" Piper cried.

Gerry looked uncomfortable, as if he really didn't want to be telling them this. *Good,* Phoebe thought, *the spell's working.* "I told her my crew wouldn't clean up the sewage spill at the club," Gerry said. "But technically it's our fault, which means we have to clean it up."

"I knew it!" Piper said triumphantly. She patted Gerry on the shoulder. "You'd better get to work. That cleanup is going to take a long time."

"That's it? I can go?" Gerry asked doubtfully.

"You can go." Phoebe held open the attic door. "And thanks for the help on my family counseling assignment." Phoebe closed the door behind him, then turned back to the Book of Shadows. "I guess we should try the reveal spell again."

"Phoebe, all it's going to reveal is that Paige can't control her power because she's half Whitelighter and half witch." Piper sighed. "We're going to have to face that. We thought Paige would help us regain the Power of Three after Prue died. But it's too much for her. Her powers are backfiring."

Phoebe's face paled. "What are you saying? That we can't help her?"

"That's what I'm afraid of," Piper replied. "We've always known that the Elders didn't want witches and Whitelighters to be together. Maybe this is why. Because their children are given powers, but not the strength to control them."

"But that would mean that Paige will be at the mercy of her powers, orbing uncontrollably for the rest of her life," Phoebe said. She took Piper's hand and held it. "And it would mean that you and Leo—"

"That we shouldn't have kids." Piper's voice shook.

"Oh, Piper," Phoebe said, "that can't be true. The Elders would never have agreed to your marriage—"

Piper pulled her hand away. "This is all too much," she exclaimed. "Leo's been gone all day, and I've been driving all over after Paige, and P3 is totally flooded, and . . . I just need to be alone."

She grabbed her purse and fled from the manor.

The sound of the water pump was so loud that it set Piper's teeth on edge. But not loud enough to drown out her thoughts.

Piper leaned back in her chair at the P3 office. She'd been hiding here ever since she ran out of the manor. On the upside, Gerry had come straight here and begun cleaning up the water spill. On the downside, Piper felt like a coward for dumping her baby concerns on Phoebe and then bolting.

She knew she was being childish. But she was so tired. She'd been trying her best all day to take care of things. Her business, her sisters, her husband . . . and none of it had worked. P3 was still a mess, and she doubted if Gerry and his contractors would be able to finish all the work on time to reopen next week. She'd stormed out on Phoebe, and she felt guilty about it. And Paige could be anywhere. She could've orbed to Timbuktu for all Piper knew. Or accidentally stolen a car or something.

Piper sighed. She was worried about Leo, but she didn't want to try calling him again right now. The truth was, she was afraid to face him. She knew how hard it would be to look into his loving eyes and tell him what was going on with Paige. And what would happen to their baby.

I'll just stay here until I feel a little better, she told herself. Eventually she'd have to go back to the manor, back to being the responsible oldest sister, back to being Leo's wife. And maybe back to being a mom. But here in her office she could ignore all those things for a while.

White light filled the room. Paige appeared in the chair near the office door. She looked grumpy . . . and surprised. "Here you are!" Paige said. Then she glanced around. "Where are we?"

Piper couldn't believe it. Now she couldn't even hide without Paige's unruly powers getting in the way! "What are you doing *here*?" she snapped.

"I don't know. I orbed here," Paige snapped back. "What are *you* doing here? Phoebe's going crazy because she's worried about you."

"I'm sorry," Piper said. "I didn't mean to bite your head off. I'm just . . ."

"Scared?" Paige finished Piper's thought for her.

Piper nodded.

"Well, get over it," Paige said. "Because I'm scared too. And I need my big sister."

Piper felt a wave of annoyance. "See, that's the problem!" she cried. "Do you know how it feels to have everyone need you all the time? I mean, I'm sorry, I know you have a problem, but I'm dealing with stuff of my own too—"

"Because you think you and Leo shouldn't have children." Paige interrupted her. "Phoebe told me."

"Oh." Piper didn't know what to say. All of a sudden she felt like the most selfish person on earth. "It's just . . . I think I might be pregnant."

"What?" Paige cried.

"I'm not sure yet," Piper said. "I was going to buy a home test today, but then . . ."

"Then my powers went crazy and you had to spend all day dealing with my problems," Paige again finished for her. "I'm sorry."

"It's okay," Piper said. "But your orbing is freaking me out a little. Now I'm kind of hoping I'm *not* pregnant."

"You think my powers are going crazy because I'm not a complete witch," Paige said. "Or a complete Whitelighter."

Piper nodded. "You're a half-and-half. And so are your powers. Other witches can't orb, and you can. It's just . . ."

"Just that I can't control the orbing, because it would take a full Whitelighter to control that power," Paige said.

"Right," Piper replied. "And I'm really upset about it. I mean, you didn't ask to be a Charmed One. And I've been pushing you to develop your powers for months. I didn't know that you wouldn't be able to handle them."

"Piper, this isn't your fault."

"But it's not just that," Piper said in a rush. "What if I am pregnant? I'm not ready! Look what a mess I've made of things today. How am I supposed to take care of kids who are Whitelighter/witches when I can't even take care of my sister?"

Paige stood up. "I'm sorry, but I can't listen to this," she said.

Piper was dumbstruck.

"You're worried about yourself and your baby, I get that." Paige went on. "But I'm dealing with something really big here, and you're not helping."

"I'm sorry," Piper whispered. She knew Paige was right.

"It's okay. I totally understand." Paige turned toward the door. "But I need to get home and try to find an answer for all of this. Can I borrow your car?"

"Sure." Piper fished the keys out of her bag.

"Phoebe and Cole are scouring the Book of Shadows, looking for some kind of cure for me," Paige was saying when the Book of Shadows appeared in her hands.

Piper gasped. The Book of Shadows wasn't supposed to leave the manor! And now Paige had orbed it here just by saying its name.

"This is what I mean!" Piper exclaimed. "Your powers are out of control, and it's dangerous! There's a demon cleaning up the floor right outside that door. He could just walk in here and take the Book of Shadows if he wanted to."

Paige's eyes filled with tears. "I didn't do it on purpose," she said.

"It doesn't matter," Piper cried. "You're a grownup, and you can't control your power. But what if I have a *baby* like that? It could accidentally orb out of its crib and land in traffic! It could teleport the Book of Shadows into another dimension!"

"I know that," Paige said, her voice trembling. "Which is why I want to find a cure for this. You're scared of what your baby might be like, but I'm scared of myself." She thrust the Book of Shadows into Piper's arms. "I don't trust myself to touch anything valuable. I'm afraid I might orb somewhere dangerous at any second. I'm terrified, Piper." She began to cry.

Poor Paige! Piper thought. She'd never seen her half sister so upset. Instantly Piper stopped being worried about herself. Paige was going through something right now, so why was *she* panicking about a baby who wasn't even born yet? She was only making things worse. She threw her arms around her sister. "Don't cry, honey," she crooned. "We'll find a way through this. We always do, right?"

Paige nodded, wiping away her tears. "Sorry," she said, trying to smile. "I'm just so tired from the cold medicine, and I have a headache. I'm being a big jerk."

"No, you're not." Piper handed Paige a tissue from the box on her desk. "Let's take the Book of Shadows home," she said, slipping into crisis-solving mode. "We'll try to find a spell that keeps you from orbing outside the manor, just until Leo comes back. Then we'll send him to the Elders to demand that they fix you."

"Do you think they can?" Paige asked doubtfully.

"I don't know," Piper answered. "Maybe not. But then we'll just have to find another solution. Maybe we can bind your powers temporarily."

"Then you won't have the Power of Three anymore," Paige said.

"We'll find a way to create the Power of Three," Piper said. "Maybe we can keep your witch side and control your Whitelighter side with drugs or something." She smiled. "I don't think you can take much more of this constant orbing."

"No more drugs," Paige said. "I've taken so many drugs for this stupid cold they're making me loopy." She pulled open the office door, but Piper stayed rooted in place.

"When did your orbing problems start?" she asked Paige. "After you got sick, right?"

"Right," Paige replied. "Why? Do you think the cold is affecting my powers?"

Piper laughed. The answer had been in front of her all along, but she'd been so busy freaking out about witch/Whitelighter offspring that she hadn't seen it. "I'm such an idiot!" she cried.

"What are you talking about?" Paige asked.

"It's not your cold that's causing your powers to go crazy," Piper replied. "It's your cold *medicine*!"

Paige wrinkled her nose. "I don't think so," she said. "I've taken stuff like that a million times before."

"Have you taken it since you became a Charmed One?" Piper asked.

Paige began to look hopeful. "I don't think so. But how could cold medicine screw up my orbing?"

"I don't think there is anything wrong with your orbing or your telekinesis," Piper said, thinking it through. "You've been taking medicine that makes you drowsy. And when you're drowsy, you don't have as much control over your powers as you usually do."

"You mean . . ."

"You're just new at it. You're not used to controlling them yet.

Seasons of the Witch, Vol. 1

Add a little cold medicine, and you lose control entirely," Piper told her.

"Man, talk about your side effects!" Paige said. "They should put that on the box! Guess I'll just suffer through the rest of this drug-free."

"And when you're feeling better, we'll work with Leo on ways to strengthen your control over your powers," Piper said. She opened the office door. "Let's go home."

"Leaving, ladies?" asked Gerry, on a break from cleaning. One of his assistants was still mopping the dance floor.

Another mess that I have to deal with, Piper thought. Somehow it didn't seem as hard to fix now as it had just a little while ago. "Listen, Gerry," she said, "you broke my sewage pipe, and now the floor has water damage. I need you to repair that *and* finish the expansion on the office and the bathroom by the original completion date."

"I don't know about that," he said.

"I will tell all your workers what you really are," Piper said. "Do you think they'll want to keep working for a demon?"

"Shh!" he hissed. "Fine. I'll work nights. Farza demons don't need to sleep."

"Really?" Paige asked. "That's no way to live. Sleeping is my favorite thing to do."

Gerry shrugged. "I don't sleep at night, but I hibernate for three months every winter. I woke up only two weeks ago. It looked like an early spring to me, so I figured I'd come out."

Paige nudged Piper. "Like a groundhog," she said.

Piper laughed. "It's still Groundhog Day, isn't it?"

"It's still Imbolc," Paige said. "Maybe we should get Phoebe and the three of us can celebrate it together."

"I'd like that," Piper said. "Imbolc is a day for looking forward, and I have a lot to look forward to!"

• • •

In bed that night Piper snuggled into her husband's arms. "I'm so sorry I wasn't around to help you today," he said.

"You already explained it," Piper told him. "You were trapped in a demon's lair with one of your charges. These things happen."

"But you had a really bad day," he said. "Between the contractors messing up and Paige being sick—"

"It's the meaning of Imbolc," she told him. "Even when things are bad, you have to keep in mind that something good is on the way."

"So what good thing is on the way for us?" he asked.

"Well . . . I thought maybe there was a baby," Piper said.

Leo sat up in surprise. "What?"

"I thought I was pregnant," Piper replied. "But after we solved Paige's orbing crisis, I bought a home test. I'm not."

"Oh." Leo took a deep breath. "Are you upset?"

"I *was* upset all day. I thought I wasn't ready to have kids," Piper told him. "But if I can deal with a missing husband, a demon contractor, a sister with writer's block, *and* the orbing chaos of Paige—not to mention being a Charmed One—motherhood should be a snap!"

Leo grinned at her. "Well, then, I guess we're going to be having a baby soon."

Piper snuggled into his arms again. "Definitely."

. . . A GIRL BORN
WITHOUT THE FEAR GENE

FEARLESS™

A SERIES BY
FRANCINE PASCAL

PUBLISHED BY POCKET BOOKS